DON'T SHOOT
THE
PIANO PLAYER

J.L. FREDRICK

To Donnie—
Enjoy!
JFredrick
9/16/2023

DON'T SHOOT THE PIANO PLAYER
First Edition

ISBN: 9798627377032

Printed in the United States of America

Cover design by Lovstad Publishing
Cover photo by J.L. Fredrick

DON'T SHOOT THE PIANO PLAYER

THE
PIANO PLAYER.

PART ONE

1

A bit tattered, the leather-bound copy of *David Copperfield* had been with Clay since his time at Silver Spring, Montana. It was among the very few personal possessions he had taken with him when he and Christian boarded the train headed for Wisconsin. A gift from Clancy Crane, who had acquired it second-hand from the little book store in Silver Spring, Clay had read the novel during the long journey aboard the ship from New York destined for Liverpool, England. Now Roscoe had it, deeply involved with the story written by Charles Dickens more than five decades ago, set in a far-away land where he had actually visited not so long before, as he and Clay had spent some time in London, and had done their share of exploring parts of the British Isles. In fact, they had traveled half-way around the globe, visited Paris, Madrid, Portugal, Venice, Morocco, Israel, Turkey, India and a dozen other places that Roscoe couldn't remember all the names. And now, in a hotel room in the little village of San Carlos de Bariloche, Argentina, they were taking a break for a while, enjoying the laid-back South American culture.

"I'm hungry," Clay said.

Roscoe scarcely looked his way, taking his eyes off the pages of *David Copperfield* for only a moment.

When he didn't get any verbal response, Clay once again voiced his desire for food. "What'y'all say we go find some supper over on the main thoroughfare?"

Roscoe pulled out his pocket watch. "It's only four o'clock."

"I don't care... I'm hungry. Let's have supper early."

With a deep sigh, Roscoe gazed across the room, considering the fact that he, too, could be persuaded to fill a void in his gut. He reached with the open book toward the table, intending to place it there, but his perception of distance was a little off, and the book fell to the floor. As he gathered it up with pages fanned out and his place lost, he noticed that the impact had broken the stiff back cover, the inner board now held together by only the weakened integrity of the faded leather binding. Disgusted with his clumsiness, he caressed the damaged book, fitting the broken cover back to its original form. But there was something odd about it. He studied it closely. "Clay... there's something inside the binding. Look at this."

Clay stepped over to where Roscoe sat holding the book. It did appear as if some object was bulging the leather. "I've read that English Monks used to hide valuable jewels and such inside book bindings."

"You're kidding, right?"

"No... it's true, Clay insisted. "That *is* a British book." He took the book from Roscoe and examined the back cover. "Looks like the leather has been re-stitched."

"Maybe we should cut it open and see what it is." Roscoe was quite certain that it was merely pieces of board that had broken loose inside the leather. The volume was in such poor condition, cutting the cover stitching wouldn't lessen the book's value.

Clay produced a knife from an inside jacket pocket. "Here... y'all hold the book and I'll cut the stitches."

Roscoe did as he was told and Clay carefully poked the knife point into the edge of the cover, working it along the seam. Little by little, the dry leather layers began to separate, eventually exposing the board they covered. Cut into the center of the cover board was a round hole, precisely encapsulating a shiny silver disk slightly larger than a silver dollar, and exactly the same thickness as the board, so skillfully inserted that, until now, it had been undetected under the leather binding. But when the board split, the disk had become dislodged, causing the bulge Roscoe had detected. It fell onto the tabletop as Clay peeled away the leather.

"Would y'all look at that!" Clay exclaimed.

It was rather astonishing. As if it were something potentially dangerous, they both stared at it for a few seconds, reluctant to touch it. Roscoe finally poked at it with a finger tip, and when it didn't appear to be hazardous in any way, he picked it up, turned it over several times, inspecting the etchings on each side. Four irregular holes had been drilled or cut through the coin at irregular intervals, three of which were near the edge, and one smaller round hole at the center. They were among what appeared to be an etched drawing of some sort, but it didn't make much sense. Obviously not produced by any U.S. Mint, the coin had been hand-made by a skillful craftsman.

"So, you think this was hidden here by a Monk?" Roscoe mused.

Clay curiously took the coin from Roscoe's fingers, and he, too, turned it over several times to inspect the markings.

"It doesn't look like money of any kind," Roscoe said. "What'ya think it is?"

"Don't know," Clay replied. And then he noticed a symbol on one side; he stared at length without speaking a word. His eyes told Roscoe that something peculiar was going on in his head.

"What's wrong, Clay?"

"Nothing is wrong."

"Then... what?"

"It's this symbol." He pointed.

"What about it?"

"I've seen it before."

"Where?"

"Can't place it now, but I know I've seen it."

"Something important?"

"Not sure."

"Well, let's go have that early supper. We can figure it out later."

2

Two blocks away from the hotel, Cantata's Inn served beef steak with beans and rice, and surprisingly, some of the staff spoke English—not very well, but well enough for Clay and Roscoe to communicate their desire to eat a substantial meal. They were seated at a table next to a window looking out at the snow-capped Andes Mountains. It was October, the beginning of the Argentine summer. That seemed unusual, but they were in the southern hemisphere now, where the seasons are opposite that of their homeland.

Two men came in and sat at the next table. Dressed as typical cowboys, their speech immediately pegged them as *Americans—North* Americans. Their English sounded genuine U.S. They were discussing some ranching chores and supplies they needed.

Elated to discover real people from the U.S., Clay and Roscoe wasted no time to attract their attention. "Where in the U.S. are y'all from?" Clay asked.

With an astonished reaction, both men abruptly answered, "Buenos Dias," as if attempting to disguise their true identity.

"Buenos Dias," Clay responded politely. "We're Americans. I'm Clay Edwards from Mississippi, and this is Roscoe Connor from Wisconsin."

Realizing their previous conversation had given them away, there was no need to try to hide behind a poor Spanish dialect. "Oh... well... okay..." the square-jawed man stuttered. He peered at the two rather suspiciously, noticing their dandy attire—black suits, vests and white collared shirts and ties, complimented by shiny boots and black bowlers—definitely not ranch hands. After a few seconds, the tension within him seemed to ease. He had good reason to be cautious, but these two dandies didn't seem to be any threat. "I'm James... Jim Ryan." He gestured to his companion across the table. "Harry's from Pennsylvania, and I'm from... Wyoming."

The four rose from their chairs long enough to shake hands.

"Pleased to meet you. Couldn't help but hear y'all talkin' about your work. Do y'all live here now?" Clay asked.

"Yeah," Jim replied. "We came last year and bought us a fifteen thousand acre spread about a hundred miles south of here... run a few head of beef cattle."

"Why did you come to South America?" Roscoe asked.

Jim and Harry glanced at each other. Both wondered about the safety of this acquaintance. "We just needed a change of scenery," Harry offered.

"Just the two of you? Or do you have family?"

"Just us," Jim replied. "And Harry's girlfriend—my... um... sister... she's off somewhere gettin' supplies for the kitchen."

"Well, we just got here by train... landed at Buenos Aires a few days ago... sailed from South Africa," Roscoe said. "We've been all over Europe."

Jim seemed to be softening a little. "World travelers...

what do you do in the States that lets you afford to do that?"

Clay grinned. "I was a riverboat gambler," he explained. But I guess I started winning a little too often, and when things started to get a little tense for me on the river, I headed to the gold fields... ended up in Montana. Somehow there I got roped into doin' some stage acting. But when the leader of our theater troupe got shot and killed during a bank hold up in Wisconsin, we all split up."

"Bank hold up?" Jim said. "Was he..." His expression suggested that he thought Simon was a bank robber.

"Oh... no," Clay replied, shaking his head. "He was just an innocent bystander... in the wrong place at the wrong time."

"What about you?" Harry nodded toward Roscoe. "You a gambler, too?"

"Huh? Me? Oh... no... my father runs a mercantile. I met Clay during a fishing trip at Devil's Lake—that's in Wisconsin —and when he invited me to travel with him... well... it kinda excited my curiosity... and I figured it was time for me to move on, too."

Conversation about Clay and Roscoe's travels continued through the meal and beyond. They had just uncorked a bottle of tequila and were sipping from tall mugs of beer as the sun hovered over the mountaintops. Any ill feelings of distrust had vanished; Jim and Harry were starting to like these two young dandies. Just then, an attractive woman appeared at the front entrance. Harry rose from his chair and met her half-way across the dining room, escorting her back to the table. He pulled out a chair for her to be seated. "Gentlemen," he said with a smile, "I'd like you to meet Etta Ryan."

Roscoe and Clay stood, bowed, and offered their greetings. After all the proper introductions had been made, they all sat down to enjoy the libations.

As the evening wore on, Roscoe noticed that something was stirring in Clay's head; he had only taken a few small sips from his second glass of beer, an untouched shot of tequila sat in front of him on the table, and he hadn't said much in quite a while. His eyes would fix on Jim Ryan for a while, and then he seemed to drift off, his thoughts in some far-away place. Meanwhile, Cantata's Inn was filling with more people. Another man sauntered over to the table.

"Well, hello, Jim... Harry," the man said in a congenial tone. His eyes shifted to Etta, and it wasn't difficult to see that his admiration for her could have been considered a bit risky.

"Roscoe and Clay," Jim said. "This is my good friend Sheriff Edward Humphreys."

They all shook hands.

"They've just arrived here from Europe," Jim added. They're from the States."

"Well," Edward replied. "Welcome to San Carlos de Bariloche! How long you boys staying?"

Edward Humphreys' origin was the U.S. It wasn't difficult to tell. "Prob'ly not long," Clay replied. "We haven't decided yet."

"Got a place to stay?"

"Yeah... we got a room at the Black Rose Hotel."

"The Black Rose!" Harry said. "That's where we're staying!"

Clay announced that he was feeling pretty tired after two days on the train. He and Roscoe excused themselves from the table.

"Okay," Harry said. "If you need anything, we're in room twelve."

"Thanks," replied Roscoe. "We're in seven."

On the way back to the hotel, Roscoe's curiosity bubbled out from every pore. "What were you thinkin' about back there?"

"What'ya mean?" Clay responded.

"I could see you were deep in though about something when Jim was telling about their ranch, but you never said anything."

Clay glanced at Roscoe with a grin. "Y'all know who that is?" he asked.

"Who? Jim and Harry?"

"Yeah... James Ryan is an alias."

"Really? How d'ya know that?"

"I thought they seemed familiar somehow, and then it came to me."

"What?"

"I recognize them from the newspapers... and Wanted Posters."

"Wanted Posters! Huh?"

"Jim is LeRoy Parker... or Butch Cassidy. Harry... well, he *is* Harry... Harry Longabaugh... the Sundance Kid."

It didn't register with Roscoe right away.

"They're wanted train and bank robbers out West."

Roscoe finally made the connection, but believing was questionable. "You really think it's them?"

"I'm sure of it."

"Are you gonna say anything to anybody?"

"Nope. And neither are you."

They climbed the stairs to the hotel's second floor and Clay unlocked the door to their room. Seeming rather unusual, the gas lights were already turned on and the room was fully illuminated. Curtains fluttered in the breeze from the open window. As an instinctive reaction, Clay shook the derringer loose from its pocket in his coat sleeve, and he wasn't surprised to see that Roscoe had done the same. A hardly noticeable smile came across his lips; *I taught him well,* he thought.

A quick survey of the room revealed their personal belongings in scattered disarray. Quite obviously, someone had ransacked the room. But there was nothing of great value for thieves to take; early in their travels abroad, they had recognized the value of choosing high class hotels for their lodging, and depositing their tidy sums of currency in the hotel safe upon checking in. It was just good practice.

"Clay!" Roscoe said. "The silver coin we found in the book is gone!"

It was the only thing of value that they had overlooked. It had been left on the table in plain sight. Now it was gone, and the intruder was clearly gone, too.

"We have to get it back," Clay said. "I've figured out what it is."

Roscoe hadn't completely recovered from Clay's discovery of Butch Cassidy. And now he was certain that Clay was about to disclose some more shocking news about the mysterious silver coin. He turned to Clay, not speaking, but his eyes oozed with question.

"It's part of a map," Clay said. He rummaged through the contents of his satchel that had been dumped out on the bed. "This map," he said as he held up a folded sheet of parchment the thief had ignored. "This is where I've seen that symbol that we saw on the coin."

Clay carefully unfolded the parchment and smoothed it out on the table. It was about twenty inches square.

"Where did it come from?" Roscoe asked.

"I found it almost the same way you found the silver coin... except it was bulging the paper liner of the inside *front* cover of that same book. I'd forgotten all about it."

Roscoe looked at the place on the map where Clay pointed; there it was... the exact same symbol they had seen on the silver disk—what appeared to be a combination of the letters V and F. An arrow and the letter "N" indicated North at the top. To the left was a crooked river labeled the Colorado. Mountain ranges were named Trigo, Plomosa, Dome Rock, Kofa, and towns called Tyson's Well, Plomosa, Stone Cabin. Along the Colorado River were towns named La Paz and Ehrenberg with a drawing of a steamboat. Among the mountains were the King of Arizona Mine, the North Star Mine and others. Running north and south through the center was the Yuma Stagecoach Road and another arrow marked "Yuma—50 miles."

The map had been carefully hand-drawn with black ink, but there were numerous notations that had been added later by someone other than the cartographer. The notations indicated the location on the Yuma Road of a January 1885 stagecoach hold-up, apparently involving 300 pounds of gold that had never been recovered... as of July 1896.

"Where is this?" Roscoe asked.

"Well," Clay replied. "Yuma is in the Arizona Territory, right next to California, and not far from Mexico. That's all I know about it. But I think this map was drawn by someone who knows where that hold-up gold is hidden... maybe one of the robbers."

Roscoe was trying to put all this into perspective. "You really think so?"

"Yeah... and that silver coin is the key. Without it, the map is worthless."

"So, how do you reckon we'll get it back?"

"We'll start by talking to Butch Cassidy's friend, the Sheriff."

"But..."

"We don't have to tell him what the coin really is... just that it was stolen from our room while we were gone."

"Well," Roscoe conceded. "He seems like a good fellow."

They heard footfalls on the stairs, and the voices were familiar. Clay folded the map again, stuck it into an inside coat pocket, and cracked the door open just enough to see Jim and Harry and Etta in the dimly-lit hallway. "Jim," he called out in a loud whisper through a slightly wider opening.

All three turned toward the call. "Clay?" Jim said. "Thought you'd be asleep by now."

"Well, I would've been... but someone broke into our room while we were at supper." He pulled the door open a little farther and Roscoe appeared beside him.

"Were you robbed?" Etta asked.

"The only thing missing is a piece of silver... about the size of a U.S. silver dollar."

"Money?" Harry asked.

"We never leave money in a room... it's in the hotel safe."

"How'd they get in?"

"Don't know... maybe through the window... it's open."

"I'm gonna check our room," Harry said and hastily walked down the hall, Etta right behind him.

"The silver..." Jim said. "If it wasn't money, what was it?"

"Just a round disk with some holes in it..."

"A souvenir," Roscoe cut in, "we picked up in a shop in Morocco," he lied.

"If it's just a souvenir," Jim said, "why are you so concerned about it?"

For the first time that Roscoe could remember, Clay's poker face failed; his eyes frantically searched the room, buying time to come up with a good answer that wouldn't necessarily be the whole truth. "Umm..." A believable lie didn't materialize.

"There's more to it... isn't there?" Jim said, eyes squinting with curiosity.

"Y-yeah... there is," Clay replied.

A faint knock sounded from the door, and without waiting for a response, Harry entered. "They hit our room, too," he said. "Unless you're carryin' it, your pistol is gone."

Jim patted his coattails and recalled leaving his gun in the room.

"And so's my new belt with the silver buckle," Harry added.

"Looks like the thief has a fondness of silver," Roscoe said. "Is your friend... the sheriff still around?"

"He went home," Jim replied. "But I think we can do a little scoutin' on our own."

"Yeah," Harry said. "If we spot my new belt on some hombre, we'll find the rest of what's missing, too."

3

The search continued all night, but in Bariloche, there were few lamps to light the dark, deserted streets and only random patches of light spilled from windows, making it difficult to identify faces or belt buckles. Harry and Roscoe went down a dark street, while Jim and Clay headed the other direction. Perhaps, splitting up might get better results.

Just as dawn squeezed its way into town, Jim stopped abruptly at a corner. "D'ya hear that?" he whispered to Clay.

Clay squinted into the dimness. He could hear some shouting and the sounds of heavy footfalls at a rapid pace. The noise seemed to come from at least a block away, maybe more.

"There!" Jim yelled. "There they are!" He pointed down the street to two dark figures running, and chased by two more. "That's them. Harry and Roscoe found 'em."

Clay and Jim took off on a dead run toward the others.

Harry and Roscoe gained on their targets. Harry grabbed for one of the fleeing thieves and Roscoe tackled the other, both tumbling onto the ground in a cloud of dust.

Harry's victim had managed to break free, and was on the run again. When Clay reached the fracas that Roscoe had engaged, he slugged the bandit with a solid blow to the jaw. The culprit went down on his knees and Roscoe tackled him again, this time pinning him flat on his back. Clay delivered a couple more direct hits to the jaw, and now the bandit's nose turned into a blood fountain, his whole face as red as a smashed tomato. In spite of his condition, the thief continued to struggle, and it was all Roscoe and Clay could do to keep him at a disadvantage on the ground. Jim was gone; he had followed Harry in pursuit of the second bandito.

Two gun shots blasted through the chilly morning air; the sound distracted Clay and startled Roscoe. They nearly lost control of their hostage, and when he scrambled to his hands and knees in an attempt to escape, Clay swiftly drew out his . 45 and struck him squarely on the back of his head with the gun barrel. He fell limp to the ground in a daze.

When he was sure the thief was subdued so Roscoe could maintain his captivity alone, Clay dashed off toward the area from where the gunshots came, hoping that he wouldn't find some disastrous results. The shots had come from a .45; he knew that sound well. At close range—at any range—a .45 is quite deadly. Chances were pretty good that the weapon making the sounds was Jim's missing revolver in the hands of the second bandito. But with his own pistol in hand, Clay was ready to return fire if necessary.

Roscoe turned over the dazed hombre to his back, and sure enough, there was Harry's silver belt buckle, shiny and new, on a new leather belt around the thief's waist. He undid the buckle and pulled the belt away. Then he checked pockets for the silver medallion, but he found nothing.

Clay heard the screech of a whistle. The sounds of gunfire had drawn the attention of the local police. "Dammit, that's all we need," he mumbled as he ran. When he finally got to Jim and Harry who were scuffling with the second thief, so did the local Constable and his deputy. One of the lawmen got the bandit in an arm lock, while the other was waving a stout nightstick, warding off Jim and Harry. When the officers spotted Clay sprinting toward them, they both drew their sidearms. The Constable fired a warning shot in the air above Clay. Clay stopped abruptly about twenty feet from the others, taking it all in. Apparently, Jim and Harry had wrestled the gun away from the bandit, and it lay on the ground about ten feet away, where the scuffle had taken place. The thief was babbling something in Spanish, and Jim was trying to communicate with the law officers. "That man is a thief," he said. "And that's my pistol that he stole from our hotel room."

"How can we be sure it is your gun," the Constable said in broken English.

"It's a Colt .45 and my initials are engraved on the handle... J R... for James Ryan. Look. You'll see."

The Constable looked at Clay. "You... Senor... drop your gun!" He pointed his weapon at Clay.

Clay gently placed his revolver on the ground in front of him and raised his hands to shoulder height. When the cop seemed confident that Clay was no longer a threat, he stepped over to where Jim's pistol lay in the street. He picked it up and examined the firearm. "Si, Senor, it is a Colt, and J R on the handle."

"Clay," Jim called out. "Did you get the other one?"

"Yeah," Clay responded. "I knocked him out, and Roscoe has him pinned down."

The constable looked at Clay and then Jim. "What other one? Who is Roscoe?"

"Roscoe is my friend," Clay explained. "These banditos broke into our hotel rooms and stole Jim's pistol and some other valuables. We just hunted them down and caught them for y'all." Clay felt quite assured that they had captured the criminals that had violated their private quarters, now that he knew the .45 was, in fact, Jim's.

The policeman picked up Clay's revolver. "Is this your gun? Or is it stolen, too?"

"That is my pistol," Clay replied. "And if y'all search that man's pockets," he pointed to the handcuffed bandito, "y'all might find something else he stole from us. It's a silver medallion, about the size of a U.S. dollar, maybe a little bigger."

The Constable peered at his deputy and nodded. The deputy dug into his charge's pockets, one by one, and finally pulled out the silver coin. The Constable stepped over to the deputy and received the coin, examining it closely.

Clay called out to him. "It has three odd-shaped holes and one round hole in the center, and on one side, there's a symbol that looks like the letters V and F.

Clay was too far away to possibly see the details on the medallion. The Constable was sure of that. After a few moments of thought, he concluded that the medallion was probably Clay's property that he claimed had been stolen from his hotel room. Speaking in Spanish, the Constable instructed his deputy to take the man he was holding to the station and place him in a jail cell. Then he turned to Clay, Harry, and Jim. "I will hold onto your weapons and this medallion for now." He addressed Clay: "Take us to your friend and the other bandito."

Clay led them to where Roscoe sat on the ground beside

the unconscious man. He held the belt, rolled up, with the buckle concealed in the palm of his hand. "He's still out cold," Roscoe announced. Then he held up the belt roll for Harry to see.

"What is that?" the Constable asked.

"That would be my new leather belt with a silver buckle," Harry said. "That fella on the ground stole it from our hotel room."

The lawman took the belt from Roscoe and examined it, holding it out of Harry's sight. "Can you describe this buckle?"

"Sure," Harry said. "It's real silver with a carved horse's head with a long, flowing mane, and a star."

The description was accurate. But the Constable still seemed curious. "You are all Americanos. What are you doing here?"

Jim spoke first. "Me and Harry own a cattle ranch about a hundred miles south. We're here picking up supplies."

"And me and Roscoe are just travelers... seeing the world... and we just happened to meet Jim and Harry at the restaurant."

"I should hold you all in my jail for a while until we get to the bottom of all this."

"Oh, that won't be necessary," Jim said. "Get hold of Sheriff Edward Humphreys. He knows me and Harry. He'll vouch for us."

The policeman squinted at Jim, and swiped his fingers across his bushy mustache. The Americans seemed to be telling the truth, each describing the stolen property quite accurately. "I will get in touch with Sheriff Humphreys. In the meantime, you go back to the hotel and wait for me."

"What about our pistols?" Jim asked.

"I will hold them until I have talked to Sheriff Humphreys."

"And my belt buckle?" Harry said.

"And my silver medallion?" Clay added.

"I will keep them all for now," the Constable said.

4

There was nothing else they could do but follow the Constable's orders; it was either going back to the hotel, or going to a jail cell, and they preferred the hotel room, without any doubt. As they walked back to the Black Rose Hotel, Clay glanced over his shoulder only to see the Constable raising the bandito to his feet, handcuffs applied. He chuckled and said to Jim, "We're not completely unarmed, y'all know."

Jim threw him a puzzled expression. "What ya mean?"

With a quick shake of his wrist, the derringer appeared in this right palm, discretely holding it for Jim to view. "Standard equipment for this Mississippi riverboat gambler," he said. "I've just never gotten out of the habit."

Roscoe followed the lead and he, too, discretely displayed his secreted weapon. "And I acquired the habit from Clay."

Both Jim and Harry grinned their approval. "Well," Jim said. "I feel a whole lot better now."

Late that afternoon, a knock on the door startled Roscoe; he was reading more of the *David Copperfield* novel while Clay was napping. He jumped up from his chair and headed toward the door, expecting Jim or Harry. "Who's there?"

"It's Sheriff Humphreys," came a hefty voice in the hall.

A sharp chill slithered down Roscoe's spine. He couldn't be certain if he and Clay were yet totally in the clear with the local constable. He stepped over to the bed and gently shook Clay's shoulder. "Wake up, Clay! The sheriff's here."

Clay slowly sat up while Roscoe went to the door and cracked it open just enough to see the man in the hall. It was, in fact, Sheriff Humphreys; Roscoe remembered him from the night before at Cantata's Inn. "Hello, Sheriff," he said meekly.

"Hello, Roscoe. Is your friend, Clay here, too?" the sheriff asked.

"Yes, I'm here," Clay called out.

"May I come in?" He smiled.

Roscoe breathed a sigh of relief. If he and Clay were in some kind of trouble, the sheriff probably would *not* have been smiling, nor would he have *asked politely* to enter, but rather, might have pushed his way in as soon as the door bolt was released. "Yes... come in," Roscoe said a little more at ease. He noticed a small satchel in the sheriff's left hand and his right hand was extended for a cordial handshake. "We weren't expecting you... so soon."

"I have good news for you boys," Sheriff Humphreys said as he vigorously shook their hands. "I was in town and the Constable drug me into his station and told me all about the trouble with a couple of banditos breaking into your room."

"Did he tell y'all about the fight we had with 'em? When we caught up with 'em this morning?"

"Yep... he told me everything."

"So, are we in the clear now? Or are we still in trouble?"

"Oh, you're fine," Humphreys said. "You ain't in any trouble at all. I made sure of that."

"What about the things that they stole... and my pistol?"

Humphreys placed the satchel on the table. "I have your things right here." He opened up the satchel. "There's a Colt and a Smith & Wesson. Which one is yours?"

"The Smith's mine," Clay said. "The Colt belongs to Jim."

"How 'bout the silver medallion?" Roscoe asked eagerly.

"It's here, too," said Humphreys. He retrieved it from the

bottom of the satchel and handed it to Roscoe.

"Thank you, Sheriff Humphreys. We're much obliged."

"Aw... you fellas can just call me Ed. Any friends of Jim's and Harry's are friends of mine, too. But I'd suggest that you two be on the train tomorrow morning. The Constable is still a little uneasy with all this."

Jim and Harry appeared at the open doorway. "He's got those two hombres in his jail," Jim said. "Why is he uneasy?"

"*Americanos*... he doesn't like *North* Americanos. You know that, Jim."

"That means he doesn't like you, either," Roscoe was curious. "You're an American."

"Yeah, but I have rank over him, and he respects that."

"You got my silver belt buckle?" Harry inquired.

"And my Colt?" Jim added.

"Got 'em right here." He handed them the satchel.

Early the next morning, Jim and Harry hauled Roscoe and Clay and their baggage to the train depot with their horses and wagon. They were greeted on the boarding platform by Sheriff Edward Humphreys where he joined them for the send-off. "Wanted to be sure you boys made it here safely. Didn't want Santiago to interfere with your departure."

"Thanks, Ed," Clay said. "For y'all helping us out of that mess yesterday."

"Glad to do it," Ed replied. "Wouldn't want to see a couple of *Americanos* rotting away in Santiago's jail for no reason."

The train whistle blared its notice to passengers not yet boarded. "Well, I guess this is it," Clay said. He and Roscoe offered their hands to Jim and Harry. "It was great meeting y'all."

"If ya ever get down this way again," Jim said, "look us up. Our ranch is just across the border in Bolivia."

"We will, for sure," Roscoe said as he and Clay climbed the steps into the coach.

As the train slowly pulled away from the depot, Ed turned to Jim. "D'ya think they know who you really are?" he said, carefully checking to make sure no one else was listening.

"Without a doubt," Butch Cassidy replied. "Without a doubt."

"D'ya think they'll say anything back in the States?"

"Not a chance... not a chance."

5

After several long weeks since they left Buenos Aires on a steamer bound for San Francisco, the Southern Pacific Railroad train deposited them at the Yuma Crossing depot, which to their surprise was the attractive Railroad Hotel, as well. It certainly made searching for accommodations a simple task. Unfortunately, it wasn't that easy.

"All our rooms are filled," was the reply from the desk clerk. "You might try the Gandolfo Hotel, or the Vendome."

So there they were; three satchels at their feet, tired and hungry, and not a clue of which way to start out.

Mexico and California were just a stone's throw away, but here, along this side of the Colorado River, Clay and Roscoe stood on ground that was not yet officially a part of the United States. Yuma was a collection of the typical squared adobe structures, although looking back up Madison Avenue where the railroad tracks occupied the middle of the street, many buildings showed an abundance of American influence.

But it seemed not much different from all their recent

travels—no one on the street was speaking English. Clay's Spanish was quite limited, and Roscoe knew even less. Although they had traveled about in many Spanish speaking countries, they had only picked up a few words, but not enough to carry on a conversation.

Clay scanned the mixture of Native Americans, Mexicans, and Chinese roaming the busy streets. One after another, each pedestrian returned a completely baffled expression as Clay requested information. It seemed nearly hopeless to find someone who could point them in the right direction.

There was a young fellow coming his way who looked more Mexican than Indian, but his clothes reflected neither culture; wide-brimmed straw hat, nicely pressed blue shirt and tan trousers were neat and clean, and although his footwear resembled moccasins, that didn't seem unusual here. His onyx-black hair was neatly combed, as if he had just left a barber shop. As he approached closer, there was no mistaking his Mexican heritage.

"Por favor?" Clay said. The Spanish word for *please* always seemed to attract attention.

"Si, Senor," the young man replied and paused to show courtesy.

"We are Americans," Clay tried to explain. "No hablar Espaniol." And then with a few improvised hand gestures combined with his Southern English, he went on. "We just arrived on the train, and we need to find a hotel... a place to sleep, a good meal, and maybe a hot bath. Can y'all show us where to go?"

Inwardly, the young fellow was chuckling at Clay's struggle to communicate, but he was too polite to let it show. He surveyed Clay's and Roscoe's attire, and determined they should be directed to the better hotels. Then, with a pleasant smile he said with perfect English, "The Gandolfo Hotel is on the corner of Main and First Street." He pointed. "And the Vendome is on the East side of Main." He pointed again. "They're both fine hotels... the best in town."

Clay's face flushed with embarrassment after displaying his crude conveyance without first asking if the fellow spoke English. "I'm sorry... I—"

"It's okay," the young gent said. "I fool a lot of people that way. My name is Carlos." He extended his right hand.

"I'm Clay... and this is Roscoe." They all shook hands.

"So," Roscoe said, somewhat amused with the subtle manner in which Carlos had turned Clay's cheeks red. "Which hotel would you recommend?"

"Well," Carlos replied. "The Gandolfo is the biggest... very nice. And the Vendome... well... the newspaper once said it is the finest hotel in the whole Territory. Ed and Jack Dunne are both real gentlemen, and they will treat you right."

"Well, then," Roscoe said. He shrugged his shoulders and eyed Clay. "Should we see what Ed and Jack have to offer?"

"Let me help you with your bags," Carlos said. He grasped the handle of the third satchel. "I'll show you the way."

"Thanks, Carlos. That is mighty kind of y'all."

The Vendome Hotel with its Ruby Saloon was their port-in-a-storm. Surprisingly luxurious for a place in this wild environment, it provided Clay and Roscoe the comfort they needed after the long rail journey from San Francisco. There was no argument about the fifty cents extra for a warm bath; the restaurant satisfied the stomach growls, and the libations from the Ruby Saloon soothed the edgy nerves of the day's travel. Now they could sit back and relax. They were back on their home continent... even though it wasn't quite the U.S.; they settled in for a much-needed good night's rest.

Clay had spent hours scrutinizing the old map. He was

thoroughly convinced that it held merit. Someone had put a lot of effort into creating it—and the medallion—which still didn't have a clear meaning, but it obviously had to be a part of the map... somehow.

"You're gonna stare a hole through that thing," Roscoe said when he noticed that Clay was studying the map again.

"Just trying to think of how the coin figures into it."

"Well, even if you figure that out, how do you think we'll ever find the right place? In case you haven't noticed, we're in the middle of a desert... with mountains all around... and they're a long way off." Roscoe was still a little skeptical; he had read many stories about treasure maps... but that's all they were—stories.   And this wilderness that began at the edge of town was bigger than he could imagine. This seemed like a task more complicated than he and Clay were prepared for.

"We just have to find somebody we can trust," Clay said. "We'll just have to be careful." His determination wouldn't waver.

The next morning, the desk clerk wasn't much help in answering their questions about a more precise location of the area depicted on their map. "I'm from Ohio," he said. "I've only been here a couple of months... but you could talk to Jack in the saloon. He might be able to help you."

"Thank you," Roscoe told him. He and Clay headed for the bar.

"D'ya think we should be showing the map to anybody?" Roscoe asked Clay.

"Well, it'll be kinda hard to find out where we need to go unless we do. Besides... we don't have to mention anything about the silver coin. Don't think we have to worry... yet."

Just inside the entrance to the Ruby Saloon, Clay and

Roscoe stopped, eyed the bartender behind the impressively carved and highly polished bar, the pride and joy of the Vendome Hotel. Roscoe leaned toward Clay and whispered, "D'ya think we can trust *him*?"

Clay studied the distinguished gentleman behind the bar— a typical barkeep—white shirt, sleeve garters, white apron, neatly combed hair.

"You boys lookin' for some breakfast?" the barman called out.

Clay determined that Jack Dunne was no threat to them. "Yessir... but we'd like some information, too."

"What kind of information you looking for?"

Clay sauntered over to the bar; Roscoe followed. "We found this map," Clay said. "Wonderin' if you could tell us how to find Lava Mountain." He pointed to the spot on the map.

Jack Dunne looked curiously at Clay, then Roscoe. "You boys gonna do some prospecting?"

"You could say that," Clay replied.

The barman surveyed his visitors' dandy attire; they certainly didn't appear to be the prospector type. "Never heard of a mountain by that name."

"Well, then, do y'all know anything about a stagecoach holdup back in eighty-five?" he asked.

Jack rubbed his chin. "The man you should talk to about that is Gus Livingston. Or maybe Jim Sanderson... over at the hardware store. At one time, he was the agent for the stage line."

"Is that how we'd get to where we need to go? By stagecoach?"

"There are several stage lines running in the Territory. But if it was me," Jack replied, "I'd take a steamer to Castle Dome Landing or Ehrenberg."

Clay's expression was one big question mark.

"Steamboats run on the Colorado River from here to Ehrenberg. From there, it's only about twenty miles by stagecoach over to Tyson's Well, or at the Landing, you're close to the Castle Dome mining district."

"Tyson's Well... is that a town?"

Jack pointed. "This isn't a very good map, but right there is Tyson's Well. I think a lot of the miners go there for supplies. But Jim will know more about that."

"Who is Gus Livingston?" Roscoe asked.

"He's the sheriff," Jack replied. "If anyone knows about a stage holdup... Gus would."

Just down the street, Jim Sanderson welcomed Clay and Roscoe into the store.

"Jack Dunne said y'all could help us," Clay said with a smile.

"What d'ya need help with?" Sanderson said from behind a closely cropped black beard.

Roscoe glanced toward Clay, his eyes questioning, once again, the level of trust. Clay nodded, so he unfolded the map and laid it out on the table.

"We'd like to know about this location," Clay explained. "The best way to get to it."

Jim Sanderson seemed only mildly interested in the map at first as he scanned the information it contained. But then Clay began to wonder if it had been a good idea to even show it to him at all, as Jim's interest grew more intense by the second.

"Where did you get this?" Jim asked.

"We found it in an old book," Roscoe replied.

"Did you find anything else with it?"

Roscoe was about to speak when Clay sharply—but discretely—drove his elbow into Roscoe's ribs.

"No," Clay said. "There was nothing else... why do you

ask?"

"The date on this map... 1885. I was the Wells Fargo agent then. One of our coaches carrying three hundred pounds of gold bars was ambushed... robbed... the gold never recovered. All the bandits... there were four of 'em... were killed by a posse shortly afterwards... all but one—a Mexican. He was captured the next day and spent five years in prison."

"So, he got the gold five years later when he got out."

"No," Jim said. "Territory lawmen watched him, thinking that's what he'd do. But he was sickly then... his wife looked after him until he died about two years later. He never went after the gold."

"Well, Mr. Sanderson," Clay said. "Y'all seem to know more about this than anyone else we asked."

"Yeah... well... I just remember... that's all." Then, after a few moments he added, "You ain't gonna find it, y' know. Lots of people have searched for that gold... but nobody's found it."

"Must be hid pretty good," Clay said. "We thought we'd give this little adventure a try." He quickly folded the map and stuffed it in his pocket. "C'mon, Roscoe... let's find us a cold drink somewhere."

Back out on the street, Roscoe knew that Clay had ended the visit with Jim Sanderson quite abruptly for good reason.

"I didn't trust him anymore," Clay said. "It was just the way he acted when he saw the map. Now, let's find Sheriff Livingston."

At the Courthouse, they were directed to various parts of the building, until they finally met the tall, lanky, gray-haired sheriff in a hallway on the second floor.

"Sheriff Livingston?" Clay asked.

"Yes... that's me," the man answered.

"Could y'all give us a few minutes of your time."

"Sure. What can I do for you?"

Clay retrieved the map from his pocket, unfolded it, and held it so the sheriff could see. "Can you tell us anything about a stagecoach holdup in eighteen eighty-five?" He pointed to the spot on the map.

The sheriff studied the map for a few moments. "I haven't heard anyone mention this in quite some time."

"So, y'all do know about it."

"Sure do," replied the lawman. "I wasn't sheriff then, but I was on the posse that rounded up the bandits. We caught up with 'em in the Chocolate Mountains the next day."

"What happened?"

"Oh... there was a shoot-out. Three of 'em was killed."

"We've heard that there were four."

"Yep. The fourth one—a Mexican by the name of Victor Flores—managed to get away. But we knew who he was, 'n it was just a matter of time when we caught up with him."

"What happened to him?"

"He didn't put up much of a fight. We captured him, conducted a trial, and he went to prison for five years."

"So, what happened to him after that?"

"He was pretty sick when he came out... they said he had tuberculosis. He died a couple years later."

"So that was the end of it? The buried gold, I mean."

"Well, we were sure there was a fifth member of the gang, and we kept hopin' that Victor would make contact with him, or go out after the gold himself. But he never did either. We watched his house night and day, and then eventually his wife told us he had died."

"Is his wife still..."

"Last I heard, Mrs. Flores lived in Castle Dome... worked in a saloon, but I don't know if she's still there."

6

It seemed rather strange to go to a railroad depot to purchase tickets for a river steamboat, but the Southern Pacific Railroad office managed the freight and passenger booking on the Colorado River steamers, as well.

"When does the next steamer go north on the Colorado?"

"How far ya goin'?" the Southern Pacific ticket agent asked.

"Castle Dome Landing," Clay replied.

"The *Searchlight* leaves here tomorrow... nine a.m. Fare to Castle Dome is five dollars."

"Okay... give us two tickets." Clay handed over the money.

"Be at the dock by eight o'clock tomorrow morning." The agent passed the two tickets across the counter to Clay.

The steamer *Searchlight* was just a smaller version of the Mississippi riverboats where Clay had begun his gambling career, and where he had first made his fortune that continued to grow—by virtue of becoming an extraordinarily talented poker player—even after he fled from the riverboats to the gold fields in the west. His anticipation here, however, was quickly thwarted. Not only was the boat smaller, but the river as well. Travel on the grand paddle wheelers on the mighty Mississippi was interrupted only by a blast from the whistle as the vessel pulled into numerous ports of call. Here, though, on the Colorado, crewmen armed with long poles lined the main deck, ready to jump overboard to assist the craft with their poles to maneuver over sandbars. Sometimes this took several hours.

By the next morning, the crew finally tied up the Searchlight along a bank at Castle Dome Landing. It had not been a pleasure cruise, by any means; Roscoe and Clay were thankful to have finally arrived at their destination.

"Where did ya get this?" the man at the Castle Dome Landing asked.

"We found it," Roscoe said. "We're just curious, that's all."

The man briefly looked over the parchment and just shook his head. "Pretty poor map... nothin' looks right."

"Well, do you recognize any of these names?"

"Sure... names are right, but the map sure is drawed all wrong."

"Well, then," Clay said, turning the parchment over, revealing some barely legible writing. "Do y'all recognize this name?" He pointed to *Victor Flores* in the upper right corner.

The station agent scratched his head. "Sounds kinda familiar, but I can't say why."

Clay turned the map over again, and this time pointed to something that had been added since the map was originally drawn. "Okay, so does this mean anything to y'all?"

"Stage hold-up... January twelfth, eighteen eighty-five," the agent read aloud. He looked at Clay and squinted, as if in deep thought.

Clay then pointed to another added inscription: *300 pounds gold—never recovered as of 1896.*

The agent studied the writing a few moments. "Yeah, I think I remember something about this... but it was a long time ago."

Just then a young man entered the depot. "Hey, Tom... when's the next boat to Yuma?"

Clay looked up from the map. The young man standing by the doorway was familiar. But Roscoe beat him to the greeting. "Hey, Carlos! Good to see you again."

Carlos, too, was surprised seeing the two travelers he had

helped in Yuma many days ago. "Buenos dias, amigos," he said, showing his usual cordial quality. "What brings you here?" He advanced toward them and extended his hand.

"I think we're on a wild goose chase," said Roscoe as they shook hands. He looked at Clay and the map.

The station agent said, "Carlos... maybe you can be more help to these gents. You know your way 'round Castle Dome. Oh... and the next boat to Yuma is tomorrow afternoon at three... if it's not laid up on a sand bar somewhere comin' down from Ehrenburg." He paused, looked back at Roscoe and Clay. "And fer you two... next stage t' Castle Dome Hotel leaves in an hour."

Carlos eyed the map lying on the table. "What's this?" he asked.

Clay carefully but quickly folded the map, asked the agent the cost of fare to Castle Dome, and paid for two passengers. Then he gestured to Roscoe and Carlos to exit the building. Outside, he explained to Carlos. "We found this map hidden in the cover of a book. It could be the map to lost gold from a stagecoach robbery... in 1885... but the gold has never been found." He removed the folded map from his inside coat pocket. "The names of places on the map are around here, but nobody has been much help. Everybody says it's a poor map."

Carlos unfolded the parchment and sat down on the bench on the depot veranda with the map spread out across his knees. Clay and Roscoe sat on either side of him, hoping he could be more helpful.

"This map," Carlos began, "Is this region, for sure. But this center part..." He pointed and traced out an area on the map. "This part is drawn on a larger scale than the rest of it... so anyone might think it's bad." He peered at the chart at length, paying attention to the details.

Clay pointed to a spot that he thought must have some

significance. "This mountain," he said, "called Lava. There seems to be a trail leading to it. I've asked several people about it, but no one has ever heard of it... much less, how to get to it."

Carlos looked closer, and a few moments later he grinned in amusement. "That is not the name of the mountain."

"Oh?" Clay said. "Then what is it?"

"*Llave* is Espaniol for *key*... like a key to unlock a door. The double L is pronounced like Y... Yavay."

"Okay... so can y'all tell us how to find this place?" Clay asked.

"I'll do better than that," Carlos responded. "I'll take you there. It's rough country, but I know that area."

"But your boat back to Yuma..."

"I can catch another one, if you don't mind me going to Castle Dome with you."

"Of course not... we'd be grateful for a guide."

Carlos folded the map and tossed it to Clay. "Then I better hurry to buy a stage fare. He jumped up and went in to see Tom.

When Carlos was out of earshot, Roscoe turned to Clay. "D'ya think we can trust him?" he asked.

Clay took a deep breath and sighed. "Well... we have to trust *somebody*... and Carlos is our best bet right now."

Four other men and a young woman with a small child all crowed into the stage with Carlos, Clay and Roscoe. Quite obviously, three of the men had not bathed or shaved in many days, and the clothes they wore hadn't been washed since Lincoln was assassinated. Tattered black hats perched on all three heads at various angles. Clay thought they were probably prospectors, but he was reluctant to start any conversation.

The fourth man, however, was well-dressed in a dark

brown suit and derby, and the young woman looked as though she had just come from a hot kitchen in a long, gray dress and white apron, her hair done up in a bun. The little girl wore a faded blue dress, but her curly blonde head stayed buried in her mother's side the entire trip.

No one talked during the soul-jarring journey over the austere, rocky countryside, where Roscoe saw nothing but cactus, creosote bushes, and a few mesquite trees here and there. Once they had left the verdant Colorado River Valley, the landscape gave way to rocks, sand and gravel, and the level of comfort in that coach was something one could only imagine.

It had been a brutally bumpy, dusty ride from the landing, and it had been dark a long time when the stage pulled up to the Castle Dome Hotel. The hazy yellow light from its gas lamps were a welcomed sight, and the thought of sitting on a soft, comfortable chair seemed almost magnificent. The sound of a piano spilled out onto the veranda, along with mixed voices and laughter—gaiety that suggested a saloon rather than a hotel. From what they could see in the dim light, the two-story, unpainted structure was a mere boxy silhouette against the towering mountain landscape, but it was obviously a popular place by the sounds of the lively activity inside.

The three scruffy men disembarked and disappeared into the darkness, bragging about the enormous amounts of whiskey they would consume at their favorite watering hole. Carlos helped the young lady and her whimpering child out of the coach, and they wandered off in another direction.

Carlos seemed none the worse after such a grueling experience, but he was more accustomed to this mode of transportation. He laughed at Roscoe and Clay as they paced back and forth on the boardwalk, trying to relieve the aches and pains. "You never rode in a stagecoach?" he asked with a big grin.

"Not like that," Roscoe replied.

The well-dressed fourth man brushed past them and entered the hotel.

"S'pose we'll get a room?" Clay asked. "It's pretty late."

"Only one way to find out," Carlos replied.

Just then, the stage driver tossed their four satchels off the top. "That's all you had, wasn't it?" he said, and without waiting for an answer, he slowly eased the team and the stage around the corner to the livery stable.

"Got one room," the clerk said. "Same room you were in last night," he told Carlos. "Number seven... the three of you will fit in there okay. Five dollars."

"You were here last night?" Roscoe said.

Carlos nodded. "Yes, but I'm a little short of cash right now..."

Clay stepped up to the counter and paid the clerk.

"I'll pay you back as soon as we get back to Yuma," Carlos said to Clay.

"Not necessary," Clay replied. "Y'all are our guest."

The ground floor of the Castle Dome Hotel was mostly one big, open room; comfortable-looking chairs and sofas filled a lounge area just beyond the clerk's counter and occupied that end of the room, and an L-shaped bar wrapped around the other end, with tables, a pot-bellied stove, and an upright piano. Another room past the bar contained a billiard table, roulette wheel, blackjack, poker and faro tables. That was where most of the action seemed to be, although the bar was doing its fair share of business, too.

Clay had his eyes fixed on the gambling hall as they headed toward the stairway to the second floor. Most of the players were evidently miners letting their gold dust and nuggets slip into the hands of those who were highly-skilled in such matters. Roscoe noticed Clay's interest. He grabbed Clay's arm and urged him up the stairs.

In their room they could hear the tinkling piano, and the chatter from the gambling hall downstairs. To Clay, it seemed reminiscent of the hotels in the Black Hills and Montana gold fields... just on a slightly smaller scale. But he knew he couldn't allow himself to get caught up in that now. Something bigger was at stake... waiting for them out in the mountains. He had to stay focused.

7

They had already walked many miles when Roscoe took notice that the mountains where they were headed didn't seem any closer than when they left Castle Dome City. "How much farther is it?" he asked Carlos.

"We should make it there by nightfall," Carlos replied.

Roscoe fished out his pocket watch; it was only 8:30... two hours since their departure from the hotel. He looked down at his boots that were now shrouded in a thick layer of dust. It was going to be a long day.

By noon, the trio had been out of the shadow of Castle Dome Mountain for a couple of hours; the sun baked everything in sight. Even in December, the Arizona desert seemed warm to Clay and Roscoe; Carlos appeared unaffected by the heat, well-accustomed to this harsh environment that he had known his entire life.

Stopping only for a bite to eat in the shade of a small clump of mesquites, they pressed on through the afternoon, following the valley as it snaked between two mountain ranges. Every few miles, Carlos briefly studied the map and gazed at the jagged mountain peaks to make sure they were heading in the right direction. There was no trail to speak of, as Clay had expected from what he saw on the map. But Carlos easily found the least treacherous path to follow over the rock-strewn landscape.

"Are you sure we're not lost?" Roscoe inquired, making certain that he didn't show any anxiety in his voice.

"Have no fear," Carlos said. "I have been here before. I have always found my way back home... eventually." He grinned in such a way that Clay knew he was teasing Roscoe.

But Roscoe couldn't help but feel a little intimidated by the rugged terrain and the towering mountain peaks. They had twisted and turned, climbed over ridges and crossed countless washes and arroyos. Now that the sun was behind them, slowly dipping behind the mountains, it was the only indication that gave Roscoe any sense of direction at all.

"There's a wash up ahead with a sandy bottom," Carlos explained. "That will be a good place to camp for the night."

"Then... we must be almost there," Clay said. A resting place was a welcomed thought.

"Almost," replied Carlos. He knew it was another four or five miles, but he kept that to himself. "But it will be warmer overnight here in the valley than if we start climbing."

When they reached the wash, it was just as Carlos had described: soft sand at the bottom of what appeared to be a dry creek bed would provide a comfortable place to sleep.

Carlos was the first to rid himself of his backpack. Clay and Roscoe merely dropped to their knees in the sand, and then settled back against their packs. They were exhausted.

"After a good night's sleep," Carlos said, "the second day is always easier."

Roscoe glared at the guide. "Second *day?*"

"How much farther?" Clay asked.

Trying to avoid causing any alarm, Carlos simply said, "just a little farther." Then, to get their minds off distance, he said, "Let's get a fire started and have some supper."

Clay managed to muster a little ambition and helped Carlos gather some dry mesquite branches while Roscoe scooped out a shallow pit in the sand, and within a short time they were sitting around a blazing little campfire. Surprisingly, the warmth from the fire felt comforting, as the temperature had dropped dramatically after the sun dipped below the horizon. It was a condition that Roscoe and Clay were slowly getting accustomed to during the short time since they had arrived in the Arizona Territory.

Darkness consumed their surroundings as they ate the hot beans and dry biscuits; sudden awareness that they were in the only light given off by the fire startled Roscoe.

Carlos noticed. "Don't be afraid, my friend. Look up to the heavens." He pointed to the sky.

Overhead, a spectacular array of stars sparkled, and then a full, dazzling moon poked up over the mountain peak to the east. It was, perhaps, the most astounding night sky Roscoe and Clay had ever observed.

"Amazing... isn't it?" Carlos said. "It's always better out here."

Just then, the yelping of coyotes pierced the night.

Again, Roscoe glanced at Carlos with a look of concern.

"Don't worry... they won't bother us. They are just celebrating the moon and preparing for the hunt."

Clay was already cocooned in his blanket, unconcerned about the night sounds, prepared for much-needed rest.

Just before dawn, with the mountains bathed in waning moonlight, the coyote yelping began again, maturing to sustained howls that woke the three adventurers from their slumber. The previous night's fire was only a mound of gray ashes in the sand. Crisp and cold, the mountain air caressed their bare faces. It would be several hours before the hot sun would emerge from behind the mountains. But the chilly morning air did plenty to get them all moving. After relieving their bladders, Carlos gathered more wood and they were soon enjoying a bacon and beans breakfast.

With all the gear bundled up again, packs on their backs, Carlos asked, "Are you two ready to climb a mountain?"

Clay—especially Clay—was now feeling a little excitement about this final approach to the lost treasure. "Lead the way!" he said, and followed Carlos out of the wash. Roscoe fell into line behind Clay. He felt good after a long, sound sleep, and just like Clay, the renewed energy brought on a exhilarating rush of enthusiasm.

The rest of the distance proved to be mostly a gradual climb that became steeper, and then Carlos stopped. He scanned the various peaks that surrounded them, pulled the map from his pocket and carefully unfolded it, protecting it from a brisk breeze. He pointed to the peak just ahead of them. "There it is," he said to Clay.

The climb wasn't difficult, but Clay wondered how a strongbox weighing 300 pounds could be carried to such a place as this. "Are you sure this is it?" he asked Carlos.

Carlos pointed to another peak adjacent to the trail they were on. At the top of a shear rock wall, Clay saw the large petroglyph of a bird with spread wings carved into the vertical surface.

"That's how I know we're in the right place," Carlos said. He took out the map again and pointed out the marking. It was a detail that Clay had missed, and Roscoe had to admit that he had not noticed it, either.

"I remember seeing that bird long ago, and that's why I was sure I could take you to the spot where you wanted to go."

"Where did it come from? Who put it there?" Roscoe asked.

"Hard to say," replied Carlos. "My guess is that it was put there by tribesmen long before our time. Maybe a marker to show the way to a ceremonial ground... maybe the very peak we are going to."

"So... it doesn't have anything to do with *our* treasure?"

"No... not likely."

They were only 100 feet from the peak, and they wasted no time in getting there. But the only thing to find there was a fantastic view of the valley below, and the next range of mountains just beyond it. More jagged peaks topped extremely steep walls of solid rock. Where they stood on that small plateau, the surface was mostly loose rocks about the size of a man's fist, scattered around a four-foot-tall, lop-sided, triangular shaped column of rusty-colored granite about four feet thick that was supposed to be there, according to the map. There were signs of digging and rearrangement of the stones; obviously, someone had already been there.

"Someone's beat us to it," Clay said, sounding quite disappointed.

Carlos closely surveyed the plateau, inch by inch. "I don't think so," he finally said. "He stooped down, pawed at some of the loose rocks, and then got on his knees to move more rocks. "Look... there's no place to hide something as big as a strongbox. Just a few inches down, it is solid rock. Nothing has been hidden... or taken from here."

Both Clay and Roscoe dug in the rocks in a similar fashion, and they, too, found nothing but solid granite a few inches down.

"The silver coin," Roscoe said to Clay. Then he turned to Carlos. "Didn't you say that word on the map means *key*?"

"Si... Llave is the Spanish word for key."

Clay dug in his pocket and pulled out the silver coin. "Get out the map again," he told Carlos. Carlos complied. With the parchment spread out on the ground, Clay placed the coin on the spot representing their location, turning it in every direction. But nothing seemed to make any sense.

After many minutes and no conclusions, Carlos sat back away from the map. Roscoe could see that he was in deep thought.

"What is the name on the back," Carlos said.

"Victor Flores," Clay replied. "But he's dead."

"And didn't someone tell you that his wife still lives in Castle Dome?"

"Yeah... but..."

"Then we need to go back to Castle Dome and find her."

8

Another day's walk back to Castle Dome City was just as exhausting as the walk out to the the mountain. Even Carlos admitted that he was tired. Here, at least, was a hotel room with beds, a bathtub, hot food and drinks downstairs. Here, they could assess all the information they had, and try to make some sense to it all.

When they turned in for the night, Clay didn't go to sleep as quickly as the others. He lay awake for quite some time thinking about the results of the day. There was no gold hidden at the place where the map indicated, and maybe this would turn into a lot of wasted effort. Perhaps the map was bogus... yet... the stagecoach robbery did occur, and Victor Flores did have a hand in the robbery; he went to prison as a result; that had all been confirmed. Until his death, Victor was the only one left to know where the gold was concealed. But why did he create the map? The Sheriff had mentioned that at the time just after the robbery, it was believed that a fifth member of the gang existed. But if that was true, why wasn't the map in his possession? Most importantly, was the information on the map accurate?

Clay finally drifted off to sleep with all this spinning in his dreams.

While they ate breakfast the next morning among a variety of miners, cowboys and teamsters, Clay decided to make his thoughts known to his companions. "Y'all know I had big plans and high hopes for this... what did y'all call it, Roscoe? A wild goose chase? Well, I've been thinking it over all morning."

Roscoe locked his eyes on Clay. He expected some miracle solution to their dilemma.

"Maybe..." Clay went on, "we should just forget about it and go back to our travels around the world, like we originally planned."

Roscoe stared at him, puzzled. After a long moment of thought, he said, "You mean... you want to give up? Just call it quits?"

"I guess so... I drug y'all and Carlos into this mess, and I'm sorry it turned out sour."

"No!" Roscoe said with conviction. "I went along with your idea because it was something you believed in. And just think of all we went through because of it. We were robbed of the silver coin in Argentina and we had to fight to get it back... almost wound up in jail. Then we spent weeks on trains and ocean freighters and riverboats and stagecoach getting here.

No, Clay, I'm not gonna let you walk away empty-handed after all we've been through. You can't just quit."

"He's right," Carlos joined in, agreeing with Roscoe. "I can only imagine what you've been through, but I think you'd be foolish to walk away now. You are so close to what you came all this way to find."

"But y'all saw it... there's nothing there to find."

"But the key," Roscoe said. "The silver coin is the key to finding the gold. Victor Flores put that clue on the map for a reason. No one else has ever had that medallion—the key—to help them discover the real location of the gold. It's some sort of code that nobody but us knows it even exists. We thought Llave was the name of the mountain... and probably so did anyone else who saw the map. The gold is there... someplace... we just have to figure out how the key works."

"And when we find his widow," Carlos added, "she might be able to help us."

"You see?" Roscoe went on. "We have to at least try... as long as we're here."

"But y'all have a boat to catch back to Yuma," Clay said to Carlos.

Carlos waved his hand in a gesture dismissing the idea. "Forget it. I don't *have* to go back to Yuma. You'll get lost out there in the mountains without me. You need a guide, and I'm as good as anyone," he said with confidence.

"Y'all don't mind staying here longer?"

"Don't ask me that again. I'm glad to do it."

Clay shifted his weight to the backrest of his chair, stared at his empty plate on the table, and fell into deep thought for a few moments. He came to realize how lucky he and Roscoe were to have met such a great friend as Carlos... someone they could trust. Then he thought about all the time and effort they had put into this already, and he admitted to himself that

Roscoe was dead right about not quitting. He reached for his coffee cup, took a sip, and leaned forward making eye contact with Carlos and then Roscoe. "Okay..." he said softly. "We'll keep looking."

Roscoe let out a sigh of relief. Even though he had first thought it seemed a nonsensical venture, he knew now that he wanted to find that missing gold as much as Clay had from the very start. He thought he was doing himself a favor just as much as he was doing one for Clay by convincing him to keep trying.

Carlos beamed a grin across the table. "You will not be sorry," he said.

"So... where do we start looking for the Widow Flores?" Roscoe asked.

"Many know me here," Carlos said. "People will talk to me... they might not talk so freely to strangers."

"What are you saying?"

"I will go out alone... ask questions... see what I can find."

"So, what should me and Clay do in the meantime?"

"Just stay here. I will come back to get you." Carlos got up from his chair, turned, and walked across the room to the hotel clerk's desk. Clay watched as he spoke with the clerk, turned and pointed to their table, and then turned back to the clerk. The clerk nodded in agreement to whatever they had discussed, and then Carlos disappeared out the front entrance.

"D'ya think he'll find her?" Roscoe asked.

"Hard to say. It's been a long time. She might not even live here anymore."

"D'ya still trust him?"

"Have to... he's all we got right now." Clay glanced around the room. Busy place for ten o'clock in the morning. All the tables were occupied by people eating and drinking; the bar was lined with mostly men tipping back shots and mugs of beer; a white-shirted man with black bowler hat and sleeve garters sat at the piano playing a tune that Clay didn't recognize; and through the doorway past the staircase, he could see the gaming room teeming with activity—cards, mostly, but several people were gathered around the roulette wheel, as well, and the sound of billiard balls cut through the noisy hum of voices. "Care to check out the card games?" he inquired of Roscoe.

Roscoe peered at the doorway leading into the gambling parlor. He thought about it a few moments, temptation luring him. He was not the seasoned poker player that Clay was, nor would he ever be, but he had become quite fond of the cards. His better judgment told him "no," but what else was there for them to do while they waited for Carlos to return? "Sure... why not?" he said to Clay. They both stood, and within seconds there were three men ready and waiting to occupy the table.

Entering the parlor, Clay noticed that most of the men at the card tables wore sidearms, and the ones that didn't, more than likely had derringers tucked away within easy reach. Clay was no different. His .41 caliber would fall into the palm of his hand in a split second if the need arose, and his holstered .45 revolver was tucked neatly under his coat. He made eye contact with Roscoe and quickly glanced down at Roscoe's right hand, and back again. Roscoe had been taught well; he knew the coded body language. He nodded, indicating to Clay that his derringer was exactly where it should be.

Five men surrounded a round table, engaged in poker, appeared to be in the final stages of wagering; a pile of money lay at the center of the table. Clay thought it looked to be about $100. Two players folded when the last bet came to them. The other three stared at each other a few moments, and then turned over their cards. The winning hand was a full house—queens and sevens. Not bad.

The winner scooped the pot from the center of the table. One player pushed his chair away from the table and stood up. "I'm done," he said. "You cleaned me out."

It appeared as though the other four intended to keep playing. The dealer, a round-faced, greasy-haired, plump fellow who hadn't shaved in several days scanned the surrounding spectators.

"Okay if I sit in?" Clay said, hoping to gain a seat at the table.

The dealer looked at Clay, eyed his flamboyant attire. The others did the same. No one objected, so Clay sat down in the empty chair. Roscoe leaned in to whisper in Clay's ear. "I'm gonna try my luck at some Blackjack."

Clay nodded and then looked at the dealer and the other players who ranged in age from twenty to forty, and were apparently all miners except for one who looked the part of a cowboy. The plaid shirt, hat, and spurs on his boots gave him away.

"Five card," the dealer announced for Clay's benefit. "Twenty dollar limit. Nothin' wild."

The cards were cold for Clay at first. But he didn't mind; he was getting a feel for how the others played and bet. On the fourth hand, he was dealt a pair of eights, a king, an ace, and a three. Not good, but better than the previous three deals. When the other players asked for three new cards, Clay asked for two. He threw away the three of hearts and the ace of diamonds.

When all the bets were in, $200 lay at the middle of the table, the biggest pot so far. The cowboy laid down two pair —jacks and sixes. The dealer sneered and laid down three fives. The other two tossed their cards face down, knowing they were beaten. Clay stared at the dealer without emotion. The dealer assumed he had won, and with another sneer he started to reach for the money. Clay calmly laid down three eights. A few gasps of astonishment erupted from onlookers as Clay kept a vigil watch on the reactions of the four other men at the table. The only one he felt uneasy about was the current dealer, one of the miners, who had won the last two hands, and who had just been thwarted. He slowly withdrew his hands from hovering over the money as Clay reached toward it.

The cowboy stood up. "I'm out," he said and walked toward the barroom. Then Roscoe leaned down to whisper in Clay's ear. "Carlos just came back."

Clay straightened the bills and gathered the coins. "Now, if you gentlemen will excuse me, I have some urgent business to attend to." He stuffed the money in his coat pocket and slowly stood up from his chair. The intimidating .45 at his hip was now clearly visible, purposely, to discourage any ill thoughts from around the table. He and Roscoe headed for the main hall.

When Carlos did not see them at the dining tables or the bar, he headed to the stairs, thinking Clay and Roscoe had returned to the hotel room. They had just stepped out of the gambling hall when he reached the staircase. "Ah... there you are," he greeted them.

"Did y'all have any luck?" Clay asked.

Carlos nodded, and then gestured to the stairs, urging Clay and Roscoe to go to their room for a more private conversation. Behind a closed door, he explained, "I asked around, and I found out about Lolita Flores."

Clay took off his jacket and sat in a chair. Roscoe stood by the window looking out over the town that was merely a scattering of unpainted buildings—some just shacks—over a large area. "Is she still here?" he asked.

"She has a cabin about a quarter-mile up the stagecoach road. She works at the Mercantile mornings, and the Flora Temple Bar some nights."

Roscoe pulled out his watch. "It's almost noon."

"If we go right now," Carlos said, "she might still be at the Mercantile."

9

"Lolita left about ten minutes ago," the store owner explained.

"Was she on her way home?" Carlos inquired.

"Don't rightly know... prob'ly. You a friend of hers?"

"Sort of... we've met." Carlos thanked the storekeeper and returned to the veranda where he had instructed Clay and Roscoe to wait.

"Well?" Clay said. "Is Mrs. Flores here?"

"No... she left a little while ago. She might be at her cabin."

"Y'all know where it is?"

"I think so."

They walked up the stage road toward the pass until they saw the small cabin about a hundred feet back from the trail, unpainted, single story, about twenty feet square. A gigantic saguaro cactus flanked the building, towering ten feet above the roof peak. Not far from the front door was a ring of mortared rocks and a windlass with a wooden bucket attached to its rope, obviously a well. Nothing else.

"That's it," Carlos said.

They followed a pathway from the road to the house. Carlos stepped up onto the stoop and knocked on the door. A few moments passed, and the door opened just a crack.

"Lolita Flores?" Carlos said as he tipped his hat. Then he spoke in Spanish to her, and she opened the door a little wider—enough for Roscoe and Clay to see her in the shadows of the porch roof. Her features were those of an attractive middle-aged Mexican woman, her black hair flowing over both shoulders. She did not smile, although she didn't seem hostile, either, and she certainly didn't appear threatened by the presence of strangers. Carlos seemed a bit astonished with the sight of her, but he and Lolita continued to exchange conversation in Spanish, and then when he was sure Mrs. Flores was comfortable with her visitors, he began speaking in English. "These are my friends, Clay and Roscoe," he said as he gestured toward them.

She nodded with just a trace of a smile, and then invited them into her modest home and gestured toward chairs to sit. "Why are you here?" She spoke with a strong accent.

Clay reached into his coat pocket and pulled out the folded parchment. Lolita watched him closely as he unfolded the map and held it for her to see.

Lolita's eyes widened; she studied the map from a distance a few moments, and then her eyes narrowed to just slits. It was clear to Roscoe that her expression indicated that she recognized the document.

"I found this map hidden in the cover of a book," Clay said.

"Why do you show it to me?" Lolita asked.

"Because your husband's name is on it, Ma'am."

"My husband, Victor Flores, died many years ago."

"We know that, Ma'am, and I'm sorry for your loss. But we're hoping that you might help us understand something about the map."

"I know nothing about your map," Lolita scorned.

But Clay and Roscoe, as well as Carlos, knew she was lying. It was all too obvious. Carlos spoke to Lolita in Spanish again, and it was clear that he was trying to convince Lolita that they meant no harm, and that they would greatly appreciate her help.

Lolita seemed to soften. She lowered her head and put her hand to her forehead, covering her eyes and letting out a deep sigh. Then she looked up at Carlos and said something in Spanish. Carlos nodded and leaned toward her, and then caressed her shoulder with a gentle hand. "Please, Lolita. These gentlemen have come a long way, and I'm sure they will share with you whatever they find... if you are able to help us understand the map."

Lolita gazed off into a distant past. Tears trickled down her cheeks. "I will try... but I don't know how much help I can be."

"That's okay," Carlos said, trying to sooth her emotional pain. "Anything you know about it is okay."

Clay decided that he would let Carlos ask the questions, as it seemed he was a little more successful with her temperament.

Lolita wiped away her tears with the palm of her hand. She took a deep breath. "Victor got out of prison because he was sick... not because his sentence was up. When he came here, he was thin and weak... they had not cared for him properly at the prison. I did my best to care for him... fed him good food, bathed him, and helped him get good rest... nursed him back to the best he could be. But he was still sick. I knew it, but he tried to hide it from me."

"Did he ever speak of the robbery?" Carlos asked.

"Very little... but he did say that one of the other men

came to see him in prison, and had asked him to make that map."

"But... weren't all the others killed?"

"All those who were with Victor that day, yes... but there was another man—a very bad man."

Clay squirmed in his chair. "The fifth member of the gang," he mumbled.

"What was his name?" Carlos asked.

"Victor never told me his name." Lolita clenched her fists and put them together at her chest. "Please believe me. Victor was a good man... how he ever got mixed up with that bunch, I'll never know."

"We believe you, Lolita."

Mrs. Flores regained her composure. "When Victor got some of his strength back," Lolita continued, "he asked me to get him a large piece of parchment at the Mercantile. So, the next day I went to the Mercantile and got that parchment for him." Her eyes wandered to the map that lay on the table beside Clay. "There were always men I didn't know watching me whenever I left the cabin."

"Sheriff's deputies," Clay said so softly it was barely noticeable.

"So, then... did he go out to the mountains?" Carlos asked.

"No... not then... at first he worked on that map at the kitchen table for days. Then, one day he said he would be going out to the mountains to finish it. I begged him not to do it... that it would be too dangerous... that someone might follow him and kill him for the gold. But he insisted... said he would slip out at night when there was no moon... no one would see him leave the cabin."

Lolita began to show signs of relief, now that she was telling the story behind the map.

"I packed some food for him the night he left with a

blanket, a canteen of water and some small tools he said he needed. He was gone for four days. I hardly slept all that time, and I began fearing that I might never see him again." She paused to wipe tears from her eyes.

"But he *did* come back," Carlos said.

"Yes... long after midnight on the fourth night. He had been walking for many hours. His food and water were gone. He was exhausted, and he collapsed just inside the doorway.

"I managed to get him into bed. He slept for two days. And after he was rested, he told me he had finished the map... that it was inside the blanket with some other things. I unrolled the pack to see the map, and on the floor fell his tools and a large silver coin. When I picked it up, Victor told me that without that coin, the map would be useless, and that I should keep it and the map hidden where no one would find them."

Roscoe and Clay exchanged glances; Clay reached into his coat pocket and retrieved the coin. "Is this it?" he asked as he held the coin between his thumb and forefinger, displaying it in plain sight for Lolita to see.

She didn't seem too surprised that Clay had the coin. "When you said you found the map hidden in the book, I wondered if you had found the medallion, as well."

"It was quite some time later, actually," Clay explained, "when Roscoe dropped the book and the back cover broke. We were in Argentina at the time."

"Argentina! Wow..." Lolita said. "The last time I saw that book, it was on a miner's pack mule... and he said he was headed for Utah."

Clay sensed that Lolita was warming up to him just a little. "So how did the map and the coin come to be concealed in that book?"

"Well," Lolita said. "A couple of months after Victor made

the map and the coin, that bad man came to our house one night while I was at work at the Flora Temple Bar. Victor was there alone, and his illness had become worse, so he was in no condition to defend himself. Victor said the man started roughing him up, demanding the map, so Victor just gave it to him. But, of course, he didn't give him the medallion."

"Where was it?"

"On a chain around my neck."

Carlos grinned, congratulating Lolita on her ingenuity, and then a puzzled expression came to his face. "But... if the man had the map, how did it get in the book?"

"I was getting to that," Lolita said. "Victor died about a month later. But before that, the bad man visited him one more time while I was gone... told Victor he had double-crossed him... that the map was no good... threw it down and left Victor to suffer through his illness.

"After Victor passed on, I was afraid the bad man would come after me; he might think that Victor would have told me where the gold was buried. So I got that old book from the Mercantile and I spent several days cutting open the seams in the leather binding, and then restitching it back together with the map and the coin inside. I knew if it stayed here, the bad man might find it, and I gave my word to Victor that I would never let him have it. So I gave the book to a prospector... said I would get it back from him when he returned after striking it rich."

"Obviously the prospector didn't know what he was carrying," Roscoe said.

"Heavens, no."

"And he never came back," Clay added.

Lolita just shook her head.

"Did Victor ever tell y'all how the coin was the key to the map?"

Lolita looked Clay in the eyes. "All he told me was that the coin points the way, but he never told me how."

Somehow, Clay sensed that she was sincere. Had she known, she would never have sent the book away with that prospector, and now that she had the opportunity to help find the missing gold, she certainly wouldn't withhold the information.

Then it was Lolita's turn to ask a question. "How did you come by the book?"

Clay grinned. "It must've somehow found its way to a mining camp in Montana. A friend that I met there got it from a book shop in town, and after he read it, he gave it to me as a gift. I found the map while me 'n Roscoe were on a boat headed for England, and like I said before, Roscoe discovered the coin in the back cover at a hotel room in Argentina."

Their visit with Lolita Flores was about over. It was apparent that Lolita had told all she knew. They had learned the history of the map's and medallion's creation, but they had not yet learned how the key worked.

10

After they had returned to the hotel, Roscoe sensed that Clay was, once again, losing faith in their ability to unlock the secret that would locate the lost gold. It wasn't Clay's nature to give up, especially after exerting the amount of effort they had already put into this venture.

"I'm goin' downstairs to find a poker game," Clay announced. "Don't think there's much more we can do today." He patted his right coat sleeve just out of habit, to make sure the derringer was where it should be, and then started for the door.

"Don't get into any trouble," Roscoe said. He knew that Clay could take care of himself, in any situation, and poker was second nature to him, even among the worst class of adversaries. It was highly unlikely that Clay would be in any danger here.

Clay glanced over his shoulder to Roscoe with a barely-noticeable grin as he closed the door behind him. Roscoe listened to the distinctive tapping that boot heels make on a wooden floor, until the sound diminished with the decent down the staircase.

"Clay seems discouraged again," Carlos said. He, too, had noticed.

"He'll be okay," Roscoe replied. "He just needs a little time to remind himself how much is at stake."

Down in the barroom, where the honky tonk piano tunes blended with at least fifty different voices and the shuffle of dancing feet on the wooden floor, Clay sidled up to the bar between two other men. The cowboy to his left seemed familiar; the one on his right appeared to be more of the businessman type—brown suit and shiny shoes.

"Beer," Clay told the bartender. He retrieved a handful of coins from his pocket and deposited them on the bar in front of him. A foam-topped mug of brew appeared and the barman took what he had coming from the array of coins. Clay hoisted the mug to his lips and enjoyed the refreshing feeling as the cold beer trickled down his throat.

The cowboy recognized Clay. "Gonna play some more poker today?" he asked.

Clay turned to the voice that wasn't Mexican, nor Indian, but his skin glowed a reddish-brown that clearly stated he spent his life in the hot sun. After a brief moment of searching his memory for this familiar face, Clay recalled the cowboy at the poker table earlier that day. "Maybe," Clay replied. "Y'all goin' back again?"

"Naw... I done lost too much already." He sounded a bit defeated.

"Well," Clay said. "I'll buy y'all another beer... least I can do."

"Thanks," said the cowboy as they clinked their mugs together in a salute to the new acquaintance.

"That's an interesting looking coin, there," the well-dressed man on his right said. There was a distinct accent—Irish, Clay thought. He gestured toward the unusual coin. "Might I have a closer look?"

Clay realized that he had placed the medallion on the bar with the other coins by mistake. He covered the coin with his palm, hiding it from the man's view.

"Where'd you get it?" the man asked.

"Won it in a poker game," Clay lied.

The man's interest seemed to grow. "I'll buy it from you," he said. "Would ten dollars take it off your hands?"

Clay picked up the coin and clenched it tightly in his fist. "No."

"I know a gent up in Tyson Wells... had one just like that."

Clay eyed the stranger's face. It occurred to him that he had seen this man before—on the stagecoach from the riverboat landing. Calmly in a low-pitched tone he said, "And who might that be?"

Hesitantly, the stranger replied. "His name is Thaddeus Belmont."

Not sure if the man was telling the truth, Clay thought it best not to pursue this conversation.

"How much do you want for it?" the man asked.

"It's not for sale," Clay proclaimed, and thrust his

clenched fist into his pocket.

"But I'd really like to—"

Before the man could finish his request, the cowboy stood up, stepped between Clay and the stranger. "Look mister," he spoke with conviction, irritated by the interruption. "My friend told you it ain't for sale. I'd appreciate it if you'd shut up and let us drink our beer." He stared down deeply into the man's eyes, their noses just inches apart, conveying even a stronger sentiment.

Clay noticed that the cowboy had his right hand poised at a pistol on his hip.

The man returned the stare, but eventually backed down from the cowboy who stood four inches taller and outweighed him by thirty pounds of muscle, turned, and strutted away, leaving his half-full whiskey glass on the bar.

The cowboy watched his retreat through the crowd and then returned to his bar stool.

Clay didn't know if thanks or reprimand was in order. He was somewhat grateful the man left, but he couldn't help but wonder if he had some useful information about the map key. And was there really another one like it somewhere? "What's your name, cowboy?" Clay asked.

"I'm Vince Carter."

"Well, Vince Carter... I'm Clay Edwards. Pleased to meet y'all."

"Same here."

"Y'all live around here?"

"I'm just a cowpoke... for Refugio Nunes... cattle rancher in King Valley, not far from Stone Cabin. He sells beef to the miners, and I round 'em up and herd 'em here, a few head at a time."

"Do y'all know that fella that just left?"

"Nope," Vince replied.

"How 'bout Tyson Wells? And that fellow he mentioned... Thaddeus Belmont?"

"Tyson Wells is a little town 'bout fifty miles northwest," Vince said. "But I don't know nobody by that name."

They downed their beers. Clay didn't ask any more questions about anything pertaining to the stranger and his curiosity of the medallion. But Vince wanted to know about Clay. "So... you're a professional gambler?" he asked.

"Used to be," Clay replied. "On the Mississippi riverboats, and then in the gold fields in the Black Hills, Colorado and Montana."

"But no more?"

"Some friends convinced me to stop... before I got killed by someone quicker on the draw." Clay glanced at Vince and grinned. "But I still enjoy a game now 'n then."

"So... if ya used to be a gambler... but ya don't no more... what ya do now?"

"Me and my good friend Roscoe have been traveling 'round the world. Don't know exactly what I'll do next."

"Some owlhoot with an Irish accent down in the bar just tried to get the medallion away from me," Clay told Roscoe and Carlos.

"Who?"

"It was that brown suit fella that was on the stagecoach with us from the riverboat landing. He offered to buy it for ten dollars."

Roscoe thought a moment. "Oh, yeah, I remember him... the guy in a brown suit."

"That's him... and he also said he knows somebody in Tyson Wells that has a silver medallion just like this one."

"What?" Roscoe said. "You showed it to him?"

"No. I accidentally put it on the bar with some other coins

from my pocket... and he just happened to see it. Carlos... do y'all know anybody in Tyson Wells?"

"A few... did he give a name?"

"Yeah... Belmont... Thaddeus Belmont."

"Doesn't sound familiar."

"D'ya think we should go there to find him?" Roscoe asked.

"First," Clay replied, "I think we should talk to the Widow Flores again... ask her if she thinks Victor could've made more than one of the keys."

"If there is another one," Carlos said, "it is possible that the gold has already been found."

"It's *possible*... but I think Mr. Brown Suit was bluffing about another key and Thaddeus Belmont."

"Well," Roscoe said. "You sure know a bluff when you see one."

"But how can you be sure?" Carlos asked.

"That's why I think we need to talk to Mrs. Flores again."

"I'll see if I can find her again tomorrow."

"Why don't we find her tonight? Y'all said she works nights at a saloon."

"The Flora Temple Bar," Carlos said.

11

The sun was sinking low in the west. Miners leaving their toils behind at the end of the day made their way to the meager shacks, some to bunkhouses, and some to the saloons. With so many active mines in the immediate area, all of Castle Dome was stirring at this time of day.

"Okay," Clay said. "There's s'posed to be five saloons here. How do we find the Flora Temple?"

"I know where it is," Carlos said. He pointed. "It's this way."

Halfway there, they passed by two dusty, dirty men who obviously had just finished their shift in the mine. They were engaged in a violent argument, but they spoke Spanish, so Roscoe and Clay had no idea what the dispute was about. Carlos urged them to give a wide berth and not interfere.

"Do you know those men?" Roscoe asked after they were well past the confrontation.

"One is Manuel Santaural," Carlos replied. "I don't know the other one."

"What were they arguing about?"

"I think that fellow owes money to Manuel."

They had been at the Flora Temple only a few minutes—long enough to realize that Lolita wasn't there—when the two slovenly men they had seen arguing stomped into the barroom. By the angry expressions they both displayed, the dispute had not yet been entirely settled. Manuel brushed past Clay to get to the bar, and the other one was pushing patrons aside to take a position next to Manuel. They both ordered whiskey.

"As long as we're here," Clay said, barely making himself heard to Roscoe and Carlos in the noisy room, "let's have a cold beer."

As they sipped the beer, they couldn't help but notice the two men getting quite inebriated, slamming down one shot of whiskey after another. It was only by chance that Clay caught the glitter of a shiny knife blade in the corner of his eye just before it sank deeply into Manuel's chest. The next time he saw it, it was covered with blood, still in the other man's hand. Manuel collapsed onto the floor. Screams of terror filled the room as everyone backed away from the man holding the bloody knife, his bushy mustache, stubble beard, dark, beady eyes, gangly black hair under a tattered hat all seemed to gloat with pride of this dastardly deed. Before anyone could fully comprehend what had just happened, the man bolted for the door, shoving people out of his way to make his escape. He disappeared into the night.

The piano music stopped. The entire crowd stood silent and stunned when it was realized that a brutal crime had just occurred in their midst. Several men crouched on the floor next to Manuel, but there was nothing they could do to save him. The blade had pierced his heart; he was dead before he hit the floor.

A few men hurried out the door in pursuit of the murderer, who, by then had been identified as Raymon Ayala, but there was no sight of him in the dark. Raymon Ayala would never be seen again.

"Somebody... go get the Marshall!" a frantic voice yelled over the murmurs that had gradually become as chaotically deafening as the gaiety had been just moments before.

"We should get out of here," Carlos told Clay.

A dead body on the floor was nothing new to Clay. Neither appalled nor astounded by the sight, he agreed with Carlos; although he had witnessed the act, he didn't want to be there when the Marshall showed up asking questions. He grabbed Roscoe's arm, and while everyone's attention was focused elsewhere, they discreetly retreated to the swinging bat wing doors.

12

Less accustomed to such things, Roscoe still seemed a little shaken the next morning. Although he didn't actually see the stabbing, he had been just a few feet from it.

Clay saw clearly that his best friend was uneasy. "It's none of our affairs," he said. "Nothing we should worry about."

"We're in a dangerous place," Roscoe replied.

"The *whole world* is a dangerous place. Two men in a dispute over money could happen anywhere." Clay put his hand on Roscoe's shoulder. "We need to just put it behind us and focus on why we're here."

"He's right," Carlos said. "Sure, I feel sad that Manuel is dead. But neither him or the killer have anything to do with us."

"I s'pose you're right," Roscoe said. "But it won't be an easy thing to forget."

"In time," Carlos said. "The memory will fade." He draped his serape over his shoulders, donned his hat and stepped toward the door. "Now, I am going to go find Mrs. Flores. Clay... you should come with me."

Lolita Flores stooped over a wooden crate of canned green beans, placing the cans, one at a time on the shelf. But she noticed handsome, young Carlos as soon as he entered the Mercantile front door. She smiled.

"Buenos Dias," Carlos greeted her, and she returned with a gracious nod.

"Lolita, would you mind talking a few minutes with my friend again? He has but one more question to ask you."

"Now?"

"Si... he's right outside."

"Okay... but just a few minutes. I have much work to do here."

Carlos went out the door. Lolita went back to the canned green beans.

"She will talk to you... but just for a few minutes," Carlos explained to Clay who was waiting just outside the door. "She's very busy."

"That's all it should take," Clay replied.

They went inside. Lolita was just starting to unpack another crate.

"Buenos Dias, Mrs. Flores," Clay said.

She glanced his way and smiled. "Did you figure out the key?"

"No, we didn't... not yet. But when we do, y'all will get your share of the treasure."

"I do not want any of that gold... it is stained with sin and bad blood... I do not want any part of it."

"I'm sorry y'all feel that way... but I understand."

"What did you come here to ask?" Lolita said as she continued to place the cans on the shelf.

"I was wondering if y'all know if Victor made more than one medallion."

Lolita stood upright, staring at Clay. "I don't know, but I don't think so. I only saw the one... the one you have."

"Do y'all know the name Thaddeus Belmont?"

Lolita thought a moment, with a peculiar expression on her face. "No... that name means nothing to me."

Clay and Carlos exchanged glances, and then thanked Lolita for her time. She went back to stocking the shelf and Clay and Carlos left.

As they walked back to the hotel, Carlos asked, "Do you think she is telling the truth?"

"She seemed pretty sincere. But she could be hiding something."

Roscoe looked up from his book when Clay and Carlos returned. He was trying his best to regain his composure after the miserable experience the previous night. "What did you find out?"

"That he probably made only one medallion."

"And what about Thaddeus Belmont?"

"She *said* she doesn't know anybody by that name."

"So... what should we do now? Go to Tyson Wells?"

"I don't know," Clay said as he slowly paced back and forth across the room.

"I know it's not my decision to make," Carlos offered as he sat down at the table across from Roscoe. "But may I give you a suggestion?"

Clay stopped pacing and eyed Carlos. "Go ahead."

"As I see it," Carlos began, "the second medallion and Thaddeus Belmont might not even exist. You may be right about the fellow down in the bar—he could be just bluffing. So, going to Tyson Wells may very well be a waste of time. Besides... it's a long two-day's ride by stage."

"But Mr. Brown-Suit-and-Shiny-Shoes must've known about the medallion, somehow... otherwise why did he recognize it?"

"That's true, but as long as we have it, we have the advantage."

"So what do y'all propose we should do?"

"Go back out to the mountain... take some provisions so we can stay longer—if we need to—and stay there until we figure out the purpose of that key."

It did seem logical that the best place to determine the function of the key was at the spot where it was to be used. It was a long, tiring hike, but it did seem to be one good option at this point.

"I think he's right," Roscoe said. "What have we got to lose?"

Carlos had one more good idea. "I will see about getting a pack mule... so we don't have to carry everything. It will make the trip a little easier."

Clay was still in a quandary. He resumed the pacing. After several minutes, he stopped at the edge of the table and stared at Carlos. "I agree that the mountain is the best place to figure out the key." He paused a long moment. "But I'm still curious about that second medallion and Thaddeus Belmont. Lolita Flores seemed a little hesitant when we mentioned the name."

"So," Roscoe said. "You think we should spend two whole days in an uncomfortable, hot, smelly, dusty stagecoach to get to Tyson Wells... and *try* to find the mysterious Thaddeus Belmont?"

"I think it's worth a try," Clay replied. "If we find him, he might provide some answers."

"*If* he exists," Roscoe said, "do you actually think he will tell us how the key works? That is, *if* he even knows."

"No... but if he gives any indication that he knows about it... or has one like it... we might find out if the gold is still out there... or if it's already gone."

"If Thaddeus Belmont exists, I don't think he'll tell us that, either," Carlos added.

"I still think we should go," Clay said with conviction.

Reluctantly, Carlos gave in. "Okay... we'll go tomorrow."

Roscoe didn't see any point in objecting.

13

Tyson Wells was another dusty little settlement out in the desert between two mountain ranges. There was gold in those mountains; otherwise, why would anybody want to live here? Other than the General Store with the stagecoach stop and hotel, there wasn't much at Tyson Wells. Prospectors with burros, horses or mules laden with tools and supplies coming from or going to their claims seemed to be the bulk of the activity on Main Street. The General Store with its large array of groceries and supplies and other services seemed to be the central hub of it all.

Clay scanned the surroundings and then turned to Carlos. "Is this all there is?"

Carlos gazed up and down the short Main Street comprised of a few adobes and other stone structures. "I'm afraid so," he said. "If we're lucky, we might get a room at the hotel for the night."

It had been a long, dusty journey from Castle Dome, and a good night's rest was a welcoming thought. The jagged mountaintops to the west were just silhouettes against the clouds that were burned crimson by the setting sun, the air cooled by a north wind.

The Oasis Hotel, just a low adobe structure, twelve feet wide and forty feet long, was separated from the store by a breezeway. Less attractive than the hotel at Castle Dome, it was a place to rest for the night, protected from the elements. Angela Scott, the proprietor's wife and business partner, smiled warmly and made the three travelers feel quite welcome as she showed them to the tiny room. "There's cold drinks and good food next door... when you're ready," she advised them.

"Thank you, Ma'am," Roscoe said, returning a friendly sort of smile. "I'm sure we'll be ready very soon."

The proprietor greeted them in the saloon. "William Scott, at your service," he cordially introduced himself. "What'll it be? Cold beer... or whiskey?"

Clay eyed the tall, likable barman, and then his companions; they all seemed to agree on beer. "Three beers," he replied.

"You gents here on business?" William said as he drew the mugs of beer from a barrel tap. He briefly studied Clay's and Roscoe's handsome attire and immediately determined that they didn't fit the prospector profile.

"No... well... sort of..." Clay said. "We're looking for somebody." He sipped his beer.

"Ah," William replied. "Bounty hunters?"

"No... not really."

William set his focus on Carlos, dressed less formally in his usual colorful long-sleeved shirt and serape. "I've seen you here before."

"Yes," Carlos said. "I rode here a couple of times with Fred on his freight wagon from Yuma."

"Ah-ha... I knew you looked familiar. Fred is due here tomorrow morning with a load of store goods," William said. "Now..." he glanced at Clay. "I was a clerk in this store long before me and Angela bought the place a few years ago. Not only do I run the store, I am the barber, saloon keeper, dentist, and the Postmaster... so I know just about everybody from here to La Paz and Ehrenberg."

"Y'all are the barber, too?" Clay said, amazed.

William pointed to the far corner of the store where a barber's chair was poised in front of a large mirror.

Clay took off his bowler hat and combed his fingers through his hair. "I could use a little trimmin," he said.

"Be here first thing in the morning," the barber replied. "I'll fix ya right up."

"And maybe we could talk some more about the people y'all know?"

The next morning after breakfast, Clay left Carlos and Roscoe on the veranda and went directly to the corner of the store with the barber chair. Bill Scott was moving some wooden crates, making room for the shipment of goods that would arrive at any time. Clay jerked his right hand to dislodge the derringer from its sleeve pocket and put the firearm in his trouser pocket, removed his jacket, hung it on a coat hook on the wall beside the big mirror, and sat in the chair. "I'll just wait here until y'all are ready," he said.

"I'm always ready for a customer," Bill replied, and just moments later he draped a large cloth sheet over Clay's torso and shoulders. He began snipping Clay's long, dark hair. "You a gambler?" he asked Clay.

"Used to be," was the reply. "Why do y'all ask?"

"The derringer," Bill said. "Saw you slip it out of your coat sleeve."

Clay realized that he had not been discrete, but he also realized that he liked Bill Scott, even though he had only known him since last night. "I still fancy a good poker game now and then, and the derringer just became habit."

"You said last night that you're looking for someone?"

"Yeah... a fellow by the name of Thaddeus Belmont."

Bill stopped snipping abruptly, stepped back to make eye contact with Clay. "Belmont?"

"Yeah. D' y'all know him?"

Bill displayed a curious expression, and then went back to combing and snipping. "He a friend of yours?"

"No... I don't even know him. D'y'all know where I can find him?"

"Haven't seen Belmont in quite some time."

"But he *was* here."

"He did some prospecting... up in the La Paz District, but I don't think he was very successful."

"How long ago?" Clay asked.

"Several years."

"So, what happened to him? Where did he go?"

The barber stood back to examine Clay's haircut, so far. "He went into freight hauling for a while, and then he was a stagecoach driver, but that didn't last long... ran the horses too hard and the stage line owner fired him."

"So, do y'all know where he is now?"

"No... I didn't know him very well," Bill replied. "He didn't have many friends... no one liked him much, so nobody really missed him when he left."

Roscoe watched with interest as Carlos jumped up and waved to the driver of the freight wagon coming up the street. The driver looked very young—no more than a boy—and when he saw Carlos waving, his eyes seemed to light up and his white teeth glowed an ecstatic smile in the morning sunshine. But he couldn't return the wave just then; he had his hands full, reigning the four-mule team in a wide turn to bring the wagon to rest in front of the store.

"It's Fred," Carlos explained to Roscoe.

"Whoa," Fred called out and pressed hard on the brake lever with his left foot. The beasts promptly obeyed the command. When the rig was stopped, Fred took off his big, wide-brimmed hat, jumped down and ran to Carlos. They slapped one another on the back and embraced in a brief, gleeful hug.

"I looked for you in Yuma," Fred said. "But no one had seen you for many days."

"I've been at Castle Dome with some new friends," Carlos said. "They needed some help finding their way around."

Just then, Clay came out of the store sporting his fresh, new haircut, looking his usual dapper self.

"Fred," Carlos said. "Meet my friends... Clay and Roscoe."

Fred Keuhn was only in his early teens, but already he was a seasoned teamster, hauling freight from Yuma to Tyson Wells. He'd started before he was nine years old, when his Uncle Mike Wells still owned the store, carrying water and supplies to the miners with a buckboard and mules. But now he made the journey—three days to Yuma and three days back—his only companions, the mules and the creak of wagon wheels.

They all shook hands, and then Fred hurried off into the store to announce his arrival with the store's freight.

"So, what did you find out from Mr. Scott?" Roscoe asked.

"Thaddeus Belmont was here a long time ago," Clay said. "Did some prospecting. But he hasn't been seen in these parts for several years."

"Okay... so there's no reason to stay here. Let's get the next stage back to Castle Dome."

"Next one is this afternoon," Carlos informed.

"Great," said Roscoe. "Think I'll see if the barber can fit me in."

Later, when the wagon was unloaded and the mules were back in their corral, Fred came looking for his friend. He found Carlos, Roscoe and Clay in front of the hotel as they were on their way to get a cool drink at the saloon before they boarded the stagecoach.

Petite Angela Scott drew three mugs of beer for Carlos, Clay and Roscoe, and a sarsaparilla for Fred.

"Awe, Angie, why can't I have a beer, too?" Fred whined.

"'Cause you're not old enough," Angela replied. "Maybe in another year. And you should be helping your Uncle Mike with the cattle instead of drivin' that team all the way to Yuma all alone... it's too dangerous."

"Awe, Angie... quit worryin' 'bout me. I make it just fine." He sipped his drink and then turned to Carlos. "You gonna be here next week and ride to Yuma with me?"

"No... sorry," Carlos said. "We're going back to Castle Dome on the next stage."

"We didn't find who we were looking for here," Clay said. "So we gotta go."

"Who you lookin' for?" Fred asked.

"Thaddeus Belmont."

Fred's smile turned to a disgusting frown. "That bastard never paid me for the water and supplies I delivered to him at his claim."

"Y'all know him?"

"Not too good... but if I ever see him again, I'd just as soon shoot him as look at him."

They all bid their farewells as the stagecoach driver hoisted the luggage to the coach roof. Roscoe and Clay stepped up into the coach that was already crowded.

"I'll see you in Yuma sometime soon," Carlos told Fred. Then, because the coach was full, he climbed up and sat beside the driver.

14

As the stage pulled up to the Castle Dome Hotel two days later, Clay noticed a small gathering at the church, and six men carried a wooden casket out the front door. The preacher led the way as the casket bearers and the other people started the long walk to the graveyard.

"Is that Manuel Santaural's funeral?" Carlos asked of the hotel desk clerk who had come out on the veranda to watch the procession leave the church.

"No..." the clerk replied. "He was buried many days ago. This is a cowboy... gunned down in the street... Vince Carter... used to stay here now and then."

It didn't register to Clay right away. But then, after a few minutes, he remembered the cowboy at the poker table; the cowboy he met at the hotel bar; the cowboy who had defended him in the confrontation with the stranger trying to hustle him out of the silver medallion. Vince Carter. Good fellow. Now he was dead. Clay was sorry that he hadn't been there to return the favor... or... to pay his respects.

But now, after spending two long days on a stagecoach, Clay and his companions had to get some rest, and then prepare for another long journey across the desert and into the mountains.

With picks and shovels, ropes, bedrolls and enough food, water and other necessary supplies to last for several days packed on two burros, they journeyed off again toward the mysterious mountain, this time with high hopes and determination to discover the secret that had been evading them. Cooler January weather had set in and the nights were chilly. But Carlos had advised them well; he had warned them of the colder nights, and so now they had plenty of warm blankets and the proper clothing to protect them from the freezing nighttime temperatures. With any luck at all, they might not have to spend many nights out in the mountains.

The trip was a little easier this time with the burros bearing most of the burden. Carlos knew that between Clay, Roscoe, and himself, they could not have carried all the gear, and *if* they did find the gold, it would be next to impossible to transport it back to Castle Dome.

When they stopped for a rest in the shade of some large boulders, Carlos had some questions. "Do you still think it was worth going to Tyson Wells?"

Clay suspected that Carlos would eventually get around to saying *I told you so.* "Well," he conceded, "at least now we can be relatively certain that Thaddeus Belmont, perhaps, does exist. Two people in Tyson Wells confirmed it."

"Do you think there is a second medallion?"

"Whether or not he actually possesses a second medallion made by Victor Flores is still in question, I admit, but if he does have one, he prob'ly doesn't know how to use it."

"Do you think Thaddeus Belmont could be the *bad man* that Lolita Flores talked about?"

"I don't know..." Clay replied.

"I don't think so," Roscoe said. "The man Lolita spoke of did get possession of the map at one point... but he brought it back... claimed it was worthless. Remember?"

"Good point," Clay said. "That man obviously didn't have a medallion."

"But we have both the map and the medallion," Carlos said. "That's in our favor."

"Right y'all are," Clay said. "We just need to figure out how to use the key."

"Have you given any thought to how you will explain that much gold?" Carlos asked. "When Wells Fargo hears about it, they'll want it back."

"We could demand a reward," Roscoe said. "Before we tell them where it is."

"But when the lawmen get involved, I don't think that will be an option."

"Why would the lawmen get involved?" Clay asked.

"Because..." Carlos returned. "There are a few people who know you're looking for the gold—*stolen* gold—and you can be sure some of them are keepin' an eye on us... including the sheriff. If he comes snooping around and finds out we've been talking to Lolita Flores..."

"Yeah, y'all are right," Clay replied. "We need a plan."

Carlos stood up. "Well, before you worry about a plan, let's see if we can even *find* the missing gold."

"Right again," Clay said as he and Roscoe arose from their

resting spot in the shade.

Even though the burros carried the heavy load, the distance was still the same, and the burros didn't make it any faster. When they reached the sandy wash where they had camped on the first trip—where they expected to stop again —as the sun sank into the horizon, Carlos displayed a concerned expression. His worried stare toward their recent path told Clay and Roscoe that something didn't seem quite right.

"Is there a problem?" Clay asked.

Carlos nodded, pointing westward. "Our biggest problem right now is not finding the lost gold."

"Then, what is it?"

"Our biggest problem is that dust cloud."

Clay and Roscoe gazed off in the direction where Carlos pointed, and saw the barely noticeable, faint brown haze.

"What is it?" Roscoe asked.

"Four... maybe five riders on horses."

"How do you know that?"

"By the way that dust is kicking up from one spot... not like the wind. I've been watching it for quite a while. And I can't think of any reason they would be coming this way except to follow us."

For the first time since they had met, Clay saw a disturbing look on his guide's face. It was that look that could mean their safety may be in jeopardy. This certainly wasn't the time to question Carlos's ability to recognize a number of riders on horseback in pursuit, but rather, to trust in his ability to keep them out of trouble.

Carlos crouched on the ground and bowed his head as if in deep thought. Roscoe and Clay sat beside him.

"They know we have the map," Carlos said. "And if that fellow in the brown suit is among the men coming this way, then they know we have the medallion, too. I have a bad feeling about it. We can't take the chance on them catching up with us."

"So... what should we do?" Roscoe said.

"It'll be dark soon," Carlos replied. "Dark enough that they'll stop for the night, too, because they won't be able to follow our tracks."

"But what about in the morning?"

"By morning," Carlos continued, "we won't be here."

"What do y'all mean?" Clay said.

"I can take you to a safe place... where they can't follow. We can't stay here. We need to go on."

Clay detected certain urgency in Carlos's voice. "How much farther?"

"Only about a mile or two from here, not far from the mountain on your map."

To Roscoe, somehow, the mountains began to seem more intimidating as they made their stealth progress through the unfamiliar, rugged terrain. In the dim light of dusk, every rock had a face with eyes glaring at him. In every shadow there lurked something unknown that was waiting to jump out and grab him. All he could do was try to ignore all the ogres and demons that he hoped were just his imagination.

Clay, though, seemed a little more steadfast, focused and sure-footed. "We'll be okay," he said softly to Roscoe. He knew his friend was a little nervous about what was happening. "We just have to trust Carlos. I think he knows what to do."

Carlos paused for a moment and turned back to his followers. "I'm honored that you show so much confidence in me."

"You are a good friend, Carlos."

Carlos gave a little tug on the lead burro's halter. "C'mon,

Sam... just a little farther."

They trudged on into the night, crossed a broad, rock-strewn valley, and then began to climb a moderate incline toward what appeared to be a towering mountain with a shear rock wall face. About halfway up the incline, Carlos stopped to make sure Clay and Roscoe were still following close behind. "On these rocks," Carlos explained, "those riders will not be able to track us." He looked back across the valley; on the far side he could see the tiny glow of a campfire. He pointed. "You see? They've camped for the night."

Clay was panting from the climb. "How much farther?" he asked, glad that they were no longer being pursued.

"We're almost there," Carlos replied.

By the time they reached the vertical solid rock wall, even the burros were challenged by the steep grade. Carlos led them along the wall to an array of huge boulders, some as big as a house, that had apparently fallen there from higher up the mountainside, but that had happened many lifetimes ago. He ducked his head and shoulders down so he was no taller than the burro's back, and disappeared behind one of the large boulders. The burros followed him. A few seconds later, Clay and Roscoe saw the flickering light of a candle from behind the rocks.

"Are you coming?" Carlos called out softly.

Clay and Roscoe stepped cautiously into the dimly-lit cavern. Inside were the two burros and Carlos standing on an uneven rock floor in a space about twenty feet across, completely enclosed on top and all sides except for the portal where they had entered.

"So, this is the safe place?" Roscoe asked.

"No," Carlos replied. "The burros will have to stay here. They can't make it through the passage, but we can."

"Passage to what?" Clay asked.

74

"To *our* safe place." Carlos handed the candle to Roscoe and began loosening the ropes that held the gear and supplies on one of the burros. "We'll take the supplies through the passage by hand."

Clay fumbled to find another candle from the packs, struck a match and handed the lit candle to Roscoe. Now there was enough light to see the ropes securing the bedrolls and packs on the second burro. When they had everything unloaded, Carlos poured two small piles of grain from a burlap sack onto the stone floor for the burros. "I'll bring them some water later." Then he took one of the candles from Roscoe and entered a large hole in the mountain wall. Clay and Roscoe watched as he placed the candle on the ground about twenty feet in. A few seconds later he returned, lit two more candles and handed one to Clay. "We'll walk through first so you can see what the passage is like. Then we'll come back out to get the packs."

He led them into the passage that soon revealed why the burros could not get through. It was only about fifty feet long, but narrow, and at one point the ceiling was so low they had to crouch down to pass. Once through, Clay and Roscoe stood up straight; above them were millions of stars and a crescent moon.

"See?" Carlos said. "That wasn't so bad, now, was it?"

To Roscoe and Clay, it appeared that they had entered a deep canyon; the top of its walls, just a vague silhouette against the darkened sky completely surrounded them. Below, a silvery narrow ribbon meandered about, a stream of water flowing randomly across the valley floor, reflecting the moonlight. They were in awe with the sight.

"Now," said Carlos. "Let's get the supplies and I will lead you to the shelter—a small cave—where we will sleep tonight. We are safe here."

15

With the feeling of safety in this secretive fortress, sleep had come easily after a long and strenuous day. When Clay woke up from a sound sleep, early morning first light was seeping into the little cave; he saw Carlos poking at a steaming kettle engulfed by a small fire about twenty feet away at the mouth of the cave. To his left, Roscoe squirmed in his blankets, sat up, and shook his head attempting to rid himself of grogginess.

"Y'all awake?" Clay said.

"Sort of..." was the reply. "Where are we?" Roscoe said, squinting at Carlos and the fire.

"Not sure," Clay said. "You'll have to ask Carlos."

"You are in the safest place in all of Arizona Territory," Carlos said.

Clay pulled on his boots, got to his feet and staggered to the cave opening beside Carlos. Most of the bowl-shaped canyon was still in shadow from the morning sun. The cave where they had slept was not large, but large enough to move around and stand up straight. Its smooth walls blended into the sandy floor that had provided a comfortable bed.

"The sun will be over the top of the canyon soon, and then it will be a little warmer," Carlos offered. "In the meantime, the fire will keep us warm."

Clay rubbed his hands together over the flames; the heat was quite satisfying, but it also reminded him of their pursuers. "Who do y'all think those riders are?"

"I went up to my lookout this morning... there's five of 'em. They have rifles and sidearms, but they're *not* lawmen."

Clay stared at Carlos as if he was being warned of danger.

"And yes, the man in the brown suit is one of 'em," Carlos added. "Not sure of the others."

"Your lookout?" Roscoe said as he sauntered up to the fire. He, too, held outstretched hands over its warmth. "What is this place?"

"It's my secret place... a volcano basin, I think. The rocks we came over getting up here don't show any tracks, so it's almost impossible that anybody could follow us."

"What about the burros?"

"I took some grass and a bucket of water from the creek up to them early this morning. They're okay."

"But won't they wander off?"

"They know where their food and water is. They'll stay."

"So," Clay said. "We're kinda trapped here."

"For now," Carlos replied. "We can stay here for a long time... plenty of water and food... there's fish in that stream, and lots of rabbits and quail. Sometimes I have stayed here for a week."

It was truly amazing—a plush, green oasis with a spring-fed creek in the desert, hidden from view and protected by the towering, sheer mountain walls.

"But if those men find us," Roscoe said. "We're like fish in a barrel here."

"Don't worry," Carlos replied. "They won't find us. No one ever finds this place."

"How did *you* find it?"

"Oh... I didn't. Grandfather brought me here. He found it many years ago... said it was the Spirits that showed him the way. *You* might call it *Divine Intervention.*" Carlos fussed with the kettle on the fire. "The beans are hot, and I made some biscuits for our breakfast."

Clay and Roscoe were quite grateful for a hot meal; they hadn't eaten since yesterday.

"How 'bout you, Carlos?" Roscoe asked. "Do *you* believe in the Spirits? Or are you..."

"Our people were converted to Christianity by missionaries long ago, but many—Grandfather included—still put a lot of faith in the Spirits, just like his ancestors did. As for me, I was raised and taught the Christian ways, but I guess I still put a little faith in the Spirits, too."

"I believe in spirits—*ghosts,*" Clay said. And I've seen my share."

"Your past is haunted..." Carlos said.

"I'm not sure that *haunted* is the right word," Clay responded. "But the time I spent in Montana exposed me to some interesting incidents and opened my eyes to some... shall we call them... *mysterious possibilities* that made me a believer."

After they finished breakfast, Carlos led Clay and Roscoe up a treacherous rocky climb to his lookout at the rim of the canyon. "Stay low," he told them, as they crawled to the edge overlooking the valley far below. From there, they could see over the lower nearby mountain peaks for miles. The bluish gray tone of the distant mountain ranges at the far side of vast, brown, flat desert plains confirmed a sensation of remoteness. But closer, they saw the campsite of the men who had followed them. They were nestled in a wash, somewhat protected from the wind and sun by a high bank on the west side. Blue smoke curled up from their mesquite wood campfire. Only three men and three horses occupied the site now.

"Couple of 'em must be out scouting," Carlos said. "Searching for us." He pointed to the lower mountain peak where the mysterious map had led them several days earlier, where they had attempted to discover the significance of the *more* mysterious silver key. The two missing men were nowhere to be seen, but the entire trail leading to the peak wasn't visible from this vantage point.

"D'ya think they know we're somewhere close?" Roscoe asked.

"Yeah, they know," Carlos replied. "They'll keep looking... but they won't find us. We'll just wait 'til they give up and leave."

"And what if they don't?"

"We can survive a lot longer here in the basin than they can out there on the desert. We have a supply of food and water. They don't. They'll eventually have to go back to Castle Dome."

They spent the rest of the day in the safety of the hideaway, taking turns periodically climbing to the lookout to check the status of the five men. Sometimes, there were one, two, or three men gone from the camped gang, but it seemed apparent that they intended to wait out the treasure hunters who they knew had the map and its key.

16

Roscoe and Clay had always been curious about Carlos; he seemed so refined compared to other young residents of Yuma with Mexican culture in their blood—at least, the few that they had encountered. But Carlos never talked about himself or his family; he had only mentioned a Grandfather. He never spoke of employment, yet, he seemed to be well-fed, happy and healthy. He and his clothes were always neat and clean. He didn't complain when faced with adversity; instead, he would seek a logical and well-thought-out solution to the problem, unquestionably well-educated and knowledgeable in many things.

So, what was it that kept him two rungs higher on the

ladder than everyone else? It seemed quite likely that he had lived his entire life here in the desert; he didn't migrate from somewhere else. Was he part of a wealthy family? He was too young to have amassed a fortune from a lucrative business, and he wasn't a gambler, and he certainly didn't possess any similarities to any prospector.

He had led them to this secret place of safety when he could have just as easily abandoned them... left them to their own means of survival in the desert with a band of cutthroat thieves following much too close. Carlos certainly wasn't obligated to Clay and Roscoe; at this point, it seemed just the opposite—Clay and Roscoe were deeply indebted to him for his guidance and their safety.

Now that they were out of harm's reach, with no immediate danger shadowing them, it seemed a suitable time to learn the truth about Carlos. Late that afternoon, when the shadows lengthened and the air cooled, Clay helped Carlos gather a pile of firewood from a dead, dry tree on the basin floor. As the trio sat around the warm little fire, Clay wanted to turn the conversation toward Carlos and his background.

"What about your family?" Clay asked. "Won't they be worried that y'all are gone so long?"

"I have no family," Carlos replied. "They are all dead."

"What happened to them?"

"My mother and father were killed by Apache."

"Oh... I'm sorry..."

"My father, Santos Volero was a rancher in Mexico. He came to Tucson and started a new cattle ranch there, fell in love with a white school teacher. They got married and then I came along. So you see, I'm not full-blood Mexican."

"Is that why you speak such good English?" Roscoe asked.

"My mother taught me to speak and read and write English, and my father taught me Spanish. He said I should know both."

Clay noticed a quiver in Carlos' voice. "If y'all don't want to talk about this... we understand."

"No... it's okay. I don't mind." Carlos paused, took a drink from his canteen, and then continued. "When the Apache raided our ranch... and some others, too, nearby... I managed to stay hidden in a cave near our adobe; it was a miracle that I survived the brutal attack. But mother and father weren't so lucky. I was only nine years old then."

"So... what did y'all do?"

"I had no one, so I just followed the sun, and after many days of wandering, when I had no food or water, when I could go no farther, somewhere near Cullen's Well, I guess, a Navajo tribesman and his wife found me and took me in, and they cared for me until I was healthy again. I lived with them for many years... until they died. He called me Grandson, and I called him Grandfather... I knew him by no other name until long after that. And I still live in that hogan."

"Wait a minute," Roscoe said, sounding a little confused. "You said Indians killed your family, but these Indians took care of you?"

"The Navajo are peaceful, friendly people; they have coexisted with the settlers, and many of them now live in Yuma. I became a part of their family, and I learned their ways. But I went to school in Yuma, too, and Grandfather taught me to hunt and fish and survive in the desert, and it was he who showed me how to find this special place. He told me I was the only one to know about it, and he made me promise to always keep it a secret."

"But now you've brought us here," Roscoe said. "You've broken your promise."

"Perhaps. But I also learned to be honorable to my friends, and you are my friends. You are in danger, and this was our only hope. I know I can trust you. And Grandfather's Spirit has told me that I did the right thing."

Clay and Roscoe smiled warmly.

"Why did your grandfather want you to keep it a secret?"

Carlos took a deep breath. It was quite obvious that Clay and Roscoe were treading on very private matters. "If I tell you, you must give me your word that it will never be repeated... to *anyone, anywhere, anytime.*"

"You have my word," Roscoe said with conviction.

"Mine, too," Clay added.

Carlos took another deep breath. "A long time ago," he began, "When Grandfather was a young man, he was with a hunting party—four or five others—they were hunting for wild sheep at the base of Castle Dome Mountain. They found a water hole, so they stopped to rest. There they noticed nuggets of shiny yellow rock."

"Gold!" Roscoe interrupted.

"Yes," Carlos continued. "It was gold... lots of it. They gathered as much as they could carry and buried it under large rocks on the side of the mountain. They went back to the water hole and gathered more, and buried it with the rest. But when they went back to the water hole the third time, a strong desert storm began; rain came down in torrents, and in a short while, a flash flood descended upon them. Grandfather had hurried to higher ground on the mountainside, barely escaping the flood, but the others were all swept away and killed."

"So, your grandfather was the only one left to know where the gold was," Clay said.

"Yes," Carlos went on. "He told the people of Castle Dome City about his hunting companions caught in the flood. But he only told his closest Navajo friends about the ola... the gold... but not how much or where it was concealed."

"Somehow," Clay said, scratching his chin, "I have the feeling there's a lot more to this."

"There is," Carlos said. "In and around Castle Dome City there were hundreds of prospectors living in shacks and tents and dugouts... some working good mines, and others just finding enough to keep them in whiskey. But one... *Long John Borlin*... somehow got wind of the secret stash of gold nuggets. He knew that Grandfather was the only survivor of the flood, and one day he pulled him into his cabin and started asking the Indian about the gold. But Grandfather wouldn't reveal anything... because of the tragedy of his lost companions. Of course, Long John Borlin wasn't willing to give up. There was a big pile of gold nuggets out there somewhere, and he was determined to find out where it was. Day after day, Long John kept hounding Grandfather, but Grandfather never gave in, and one day when he had become weary of the of the prospector's questions, he decided to just leave Castle Dome... he moved to Yuma.

"But Long John Borlin still didn't give up... he searched for that pile of gold nuggets for twenty-five years."

"Did he ever find it?" Roscoe asked.

"No," Carlos replied. "He couldn't, because it wasn't there to find."

Clay and Roscoe stared at Carlos. "You mean," Roscoe said, "the gold never existed? It was all a lie?"

"No, it existed, all right, but it wasn't where the Navajo hunting party hid it."

"What happened to it?"

"Grandfather became worried that Long John Borlin would eventually get lucky. So for many nights in the cover of darkness, he took the gold—as much as he could carry at a time—and moved it to a place where he knew Long John Borlin... or anybody else... would never find it. And he continued to gather more nuggets that had been washed down into the hole by the flood. All that water came rushing down from the mountain and carried more gold with it."

"So, your grandfather became a wealthy man, and that's why y'all are probably just as rich."

"Oh, no," Carlos said. "Grandfather was a Navajo, and people would get suspicious if a Navajo started acting like a wealthy man. So he took only a nugget or two at a time... like a prospector might do... and sold them in Yuma for money... enough for him and his wife to live comfortably in their little hogan. And that's just what I do, as well."

"So y'all have the gold!" Clay said.

"No," Carlos replied. "The mountain has the gold. I just get a little of it now an then... when I need it, just like Grandfather did. But you have heard enough for one day." He looked to the rim of the canyon. "It will be dark soon. We should catch some fish from the stream and make good use of this fire."

17

Roscoe felt right at home fishing at the little creek. Fishing had always been his favorite pastime back in Wisconsin; its how he had met Clay at Devil's Lake. Of course, here the tackle was a bit different than what he was accustomed to; Carlos had stashed all sorts of things in his little cave—pots and pans, cups and plates, knives, bow and arrows, and, yes, a fishing pole and tackle—nothing fancy, but it worked. So it became Roscoe's responsibility to catch the fish for supper.

Two more days passed; every time they checked on the five men, the status had not changed. Their campsite was positioned so they could keep an eye on the trail leading up to the peak where the key held some significance. Carlos knew of no other way to reach the peak—at least he had never looked for one. He'd never had a reason.

The men were camped at a location that would make exiting the basin through the secret portal nearly impossible without being seen... in daylight. However, in the dark of night, especially now with just a sliver of a crescent moon, it might be possible to sneak out and take an alternate route in the opposite direction along the vertical wall and down the other side of the mountain away from the five men. But it would be risky.

Carlos thought he might be able to do it alone; just one person alone in the dark was less likely to be noticed. "I'll go out tonight, when it's dark," he told the others. "I know the way down the other side. I'll sneak around to the back of their camp... try to hear what they talk about... at least, find out who they are."

"D'ya think that's safe?" Roscoe asked.

"I'll be careful. I may not be Navajo, but I was taught by one."

"I should go with y'all," Clay said.

"No—"

"But those critters down there have guns..."

"And I have bow and arrows... and I'm quite good with a bow."

Clay knew that was true—he'd seen Carlos pick off a rabbit at thirty yards for their supper a couple of days earlier.

"But if they see you," Roscoe said. "How will you get back here without them following you?"

"There's no moon tonight. It will be too dark."

"Clay and I will watch from the lookout... and if you get into trouble down there—"

"You can watch, but you probably won't see anything except for the men by the fire."

After they ate the fish that Roscoe caught, Carlos prepared for the scouting mission. Armed with bow and a quiver full of arrows, knife and water skin, he slipped quietly off into the darkness.

Clay and Roscoe climbed up to the lookout; they could see the small campfire below. It illuminated the camp just enough to occasionally identify a shadowy figure moving about, but with a moderate wind blowing, it was impossible to hear any sounds or voices. It was just too far away. Carlos had been right: no moon—the landscape almost entirely concealed. The mountain peaks on the distant horizon were only a vague, jagged black line.

"How can he possibly find his way?" Roscoe said.

"He knows this land... these mountains... this desert. If anyone can find his way... Carlos can."

More than an hour later, Carlos had made his stealth approach to the the high bank overlooking the campsite in the arroyo. He could see the flickering yellow light from the fire, and he could hear voices, but they were muffled by the wind. He got on his belly and crawled closer to the edge of the bank. He still couldn't see any of the men, but the voices became more legible.

"I don't think those greenhorns are out here anymore," he finally heard one of the voices say.

"Must be," another one said. "Tracks came here."

"But we've searched every nook and cranny in these mountains."

Carlos had never heard the man in the brown suit speak, so he didn't know if one of the voices was his. He didn't recognize any of the others, either.

"Maybe we should just call it quits."

"Go back to town tomorrow."

"Yeah... cold out here."

"But we need the map and that medallion."

"Or... we could just wait for 'em to come back to Castle Dome."

The fire light gradually diminished, and when he could hear no more talking, Carlos figured the men must have fallen asleep. As he carefully backed away from the bank, he suddenly heard the men stirring again. "Hey! I heard something," one of the men said in a panic.

Carlos pulled an arrow from the quiver on his back, noched it on the bowstring, aimed at the edge of the bank, ready to defend against an assault.

The hazy glow of a lantern abruptly appeared and then it seemed to be rising toward the edge of the high bank. A moment later, Carlos was staring at a silhouette of a man holding the lantern high. Fortunately, he was too far away for the circle of light to fully reach Carlos. But Carlos could see the sparkle of a revolver in the man's other hand. He aimed for the man's leg and let the arrow fly. The lantern crashed to the ground and the man cried out painfully, "Ahhhhh!"

Carlos backed away farther, as another man came to the the wounded man's side and picked up the lantern. "Injuns!" he heard a voice call out, and seconds later a barrage of gunfire sent slugs zinging into the darkness, failing to find any target. By that time, Carlos had turned to his left and his moccasins carried him swiftly, silently, safely away from the light and the coarse of the bullets.

When the fire had died and nothing was visible anymore from the lookout, Roscoe and Clay returned to the protection of the little cave. It was warmer there, out of the wind. All they could do now was rekindle their own fire and wait for

Carlos. They had not seen the lantern, and down in the basin, behind the high canyon walls and the muffling wind, they had not heard the gun shots.

18

Well past 2:00 o'clock, Clay heard footfalls approaching the shelter. Only when he saw Carlos appear in the firelight did he holster his .45; he breathed a sigh of relief, knowing that Carlos was safe. "Y'all made it..." he said. Roscoe had dozed off, but he abruptly came awake when Carlos plopped down by the fire.

"It was not so easy with no moonlight," Carlos said. "Did you watch from the lookout?"

"We could only see the campfire, and when it went out... nothing," Clay said.

"We came back here to get out of the wind," Roscoe added.

"So you didn't see them shooting at me?"

"No!"

"They shot at y'all?"

"When it had been quiet for a while, I thought they were all asleep, and I started to leave," Carlos explained. "But they must've heard me. I had to shoot one of them in the leg with my bow."

"So now they're gonna come after us for sure," Roscoe said, a little frightened.

"No, I don't think so," Carlos replied. "I heard one of 'em shout "Injuns" as I was running away, so they don't know it was one of us."

"Did you find out anything?" Clay asked.

"Well," Carlos replied. "I didn't recognize any voices... and I couldn't see any faces. But I heard them talking about us.

And from what I could tell, they might be giving up... going back to Castle Dome tomorrow."

"Hey, that's great!" Roscoe said.

"But we can't go back there... not right away."

"Why?"

"Because they plan to ambush us on the way back."

"So, what should we do?"

"We'll figure something out," Carlos said. "Right now, I'm tired. I want to get some sleep."

Even with so little rest, Carlos had been awake and up the next morning long before the others. The sun was already high in the sky when Clay watched Carlos hiking along the creek and up to the shelter, his bow in one hand and a fat rabbit and two plump quail dangling from the other. He held them up for Clay to see. "We'll eat good today," he said with a grin.

Clay recalled the previous night's activity. If Carlos had collected accurate information, today might be the end of their confinement in the basin, although, the past few days had not been entirely unpleasant. Thanks to Carlos. They had stayed warm and dry at night, and they had never been hungry or thirsty.

But they *had* been held as prisoners of sorts, by five men they did not know, and that angered Clay. He was quite certain that it frightened Roscoe. After all the dangers and close calls he had subjected Roscoe to by convincing him to come on this treasure hunt, Roscoe would probably never trust him again, and would want to catch the next train back to Wisconsin. *Couldn't blame him,* Clay thought.

"We should go up to the lookout," Clay said. "See if those men are gone."

"Already did," Carlos said. "Still there."

Roscoe rolled out of his blankets and sauntered over to examine the game. He hadn't slept very well, the visions of five gunmen showering them with lead had prevented a good night's sleep.

"Carlos says those men are still camped out there," Clay told Roscoe. "So, we'll have to stay here a while longer."

19

One of the five men at the camp hadn't moved from a prone position all day; he was obviously the one who took the arrow in his leg. It seemed just good sense that they would be on the move soon to seek medical attention for him, but they didn't seem to be in any hurry.

To pass the time, between trips to the lookout, the three sat in the little cave and continued to tell stories about their past experiences. Carlos was particularly interested in Clay's life as a professional gambler, how he had learned the art of gambling while working aboard a Mississippi riverboat. "I started winning more than I lost, and the night I won twenty-five thousand dollars from a cotton plantation owner, I knew then that poker was the best way to make a living."

"And he's mighty quick with a gun, too," Roscoe added. "I'll never forget the day we met." He went on to describe the confrontation with a gang of thugs in an alley and his first glance at Clay's double-barrel Remington derringer that instantly, miraculously appeared in his hand. "I started learning from him that day, and I'm grateful for every lesson he's taught me since."

"But I see you carry a forty-five," Carlos said to Clay.

Clay jerked his right hand; the shiny little derringer

appeared in his palm; he held it out for Carlos to see. "Always ready... never without it."

"I have one, too," Roscoe said, and he, too, demonstrated how quickly it could be summoned into use.

"Carlos," Clay said. "There's something I've been meaning to ask y'all."

"Okay," Carlos responded.

"When we went to find the Widow Flores the first time, y'all knew exactly where to find her cabin... and she seemed almost like y'all weren't a stranger to her."

Carlos just stared back at Clay with a mildly curious expression.

"So, did y'all know her before that?"

As if he were just a bit embarrassed, Carlos gave a sheepish little smile, nodded. "Yes," he admitted. "But I didn't know her husband had anything to do with a stagecoach robbery... and I hadn't seen her in a while. That day when I went looking for Victor's widow, it all started adding up."

"But y'all never told us."

"I didn't think it was important."

"How long have you known her," Roscoe asked.

"Just for a couple of years. I had been coming to Castle Dome alone after Grandfather died. One night, I went to the Flora Temple Bar because I heard some beautiful music— piano music—coming from there. When I got inside I saw the player was a pretty girl... the prettiest girl I'd ever seen."

"Lolita?"

"No... another girl. I didn't even know Lolita then."

"Okay... so, what happened?"

"I stayed there until she was through playing, so I could talk to her. Dora was from the East—New York, I think—and she'd come here with her piano. Her parents had died, and so we had something in common.

"Of course, everybody loved to listen to her play, and so the Flora Temple became even more popular, so crowded that sometimes it was hard to even get to talk to her. One night, a miner and a cowboy got into a fight... inside the Flora Temple... and they were both pretty drunk. The cowboy took out his six-gun and started shooting. Everybody went crazy. A couple of other men were trying to capture him but he kept shooting. I stood up on a chair and yelled "DON'T SHOOT THE PIANO PLAYER!" and it was enough of a distraction to the cowboy that the other two men were able to wrestle his gun away from him. They hogtied him and drug him over to the Marshall's office."

"So, what does that have to do with y'all getting to know Lolita Flores?"

"Well," Carlos went on. "I saw Dora quite a few times during the next several months, and I was working up the courage to ask her to come back to Yuma with me... find a nice place where she could play down there."

"But that didn't happen, did it?" Roscoe said.

"No... the next time I came to Castle Dome, she was gone. Some dandy gambler had come to town, and somehow he made her fall in love with him. They got married and he whisked her away to San Francisco."

"Aw, Carlos, that's terrible."

"Yeah, but the worst part is... not long after that, word came back that Dora was found murdered, and her husband had disappeared with her small fortune she came here with, and the money she had earned performing."

"Did they ever catch him?"

"Not that I know."

"So, how do y'all know Lolita Flores?" Clay asked again.

"Well, when I found out that Dora was gone, I was heart-broken. I sat at the bar, almost in tears. That's when Lolita sat down next to me. She put her arm around me and said that I would get over it in time, and that everything would be okay."

A little melancholy crept into Carlos's voice as he continued. "She invited me to spend the night at her cabin... she was lonely, too, after losing her husband." Carlos looked at Clay and then Roscoe, as if pleading to be understood. "She was a pretty lady, and she made me feel good."

"Well, I can see why she might be attracted to a handsome young fella as charming as y'all," Clay said. "But Carlos... she's almost twice your age."

"I know... and I knew it then. That's why I didn't see her again after that."

20

When the sun was up the next morning, Carlos came down from the lookout with good news. The five men had abandoned their camp in the valley; they were gone. All that remained was the charred fire pit.

"Before we go today," Carlos said to Clay and Roscoe while they sat next to the little campfire, "there's something I want you to have."

The two of them eyed Carlos with curiosity. Neither of them could imagine what more Carlos could possibly bestow upon them; he had already done so much.

"In case we don't find the strongbox," Carlos said as he pulled a small leather pouch from his pocket. He tugged the drawstrings loose and dumped the contents into his left hand, keeping it concealed from Clay's and Roscoe's sight. "I want to give you this." He apparently divided whatever he poured from the pouch, transferring part of it to his right hand. With closed fists, he extended his arms toward Roscoe and Clay. "Hold out your hands," he instructed them.

They leaned forward, and each held out a hand, palms up. Carefully, slowly, Carlos uncurled his fingers, releasing the objects into the outstretched hands.

Clay and Roscoe stared at the six bright, shiny, acorn-sized yellow stones they each held. "What...?" they both uttered.

"It's gold from Grandfather's mine," Carlos said. His expression was stern and sincere. "I don't want you to leave here empty-handed... if the stagecoach gold is not there."

Nearly frozen in disbelief, Clay glared at the large nuggets glittering in his hand. "But... Carlos..." he stuttered. "We can't... take *your* gold."

"Why not?" Carlos replied. "I have plenty... and I owe you for the hotel rooms... and the restaurant meals and drinks... and the stagecoach fares—"

"You don't owe us anything," Roscoe interrupted.

Carlos looked Roscoe squarely in the eyes. "Put those gold nuggets in your pockets... both of you! You're keeping them. And that's final."

"Your Granddad's mine," Clay said, "It's on this mountain?"

"That is to remain our solemn secret," Carlos replied. "We agreed on that... remember? You are *never* to speak of this mountain or where those gold nuggets came from."

21

The day was still young; they could easily get to their "key" mountain peak and once again try to decipher the message hidden on the silver medallion. Their mission had been delayed for many days, and they all were anxious to solve the puzzle and locate a fantastic treasure. Nothing was going to stand in their way.

"We'll take everything with us," Carlos said, as he began packing up his bedroll. "In case we don't come back here tonight."

There wasn't much left to pack—the food they brought in, they had consumed, and the burros had been on a steady diet of marsh grass and cattails for the last three days.

Still quite overwhelmed by the generous gift that Carlos had insisted on giving them, Roscoe and Clay just followed his instructions. By virtue of his skills and knowledge of these mountains, they considered him in command now. He had led them here, and he would lead them to safety again, although, he had not yet informed them of any plan to avoid an ambush when they returned to Castle Dome. But their confidence in his abilities continued to grow.

Even the burros seemed happy to leave their stone barn confinement. With a little lighter load now, they plodded down the rock-covered incline, Carlos leading and keeping them from trying to go too fast, which could result in a fall and a broken leg. Roscoe and Clay followed patiently behind. The serpentine route that Carlos took reduced the steepness of the climb down, but it was still steep.

Carlos led the way across the valley, past the wash where the five men had been camped, and then found some sturdy mesquite trees. There the burros could be tethered near the trail leading up to the mountain peak destination. "Do you have the map and the medallion?" he asked Clay.

Clay patted his coat breast, feeling the items in the inside pocket. "Right here," he said.

"Okay," Carlos replied. "We're ready to go."

With three full canteens of water and spirits full of determination, they started the climb up the mountain trail.

They had circled around to another side of the mountain with the volcano basin, away from the secret entrance behind the big boulders. Roscoe remembered the huge petroglyph bird they had seen on the previous trip here; he watched for it. As they neared the peak, there it was, just as he remembered. It occurred to him that it was on the side of the mountain where they had stayed safely hidden for many days. "Carlos?" he said. "That bird carving... it's there to mark *that* mountain, isn't it?"

They all stopped to peer at the mysterious bird on the mountain wall.

"Perhaps," Carlos replied with a sly grin after a long, dramatic pause.

"We will never speak of it," Clay said, returning another sly smile and a wink to Carlos, and then urged them to continue the hike up to the peak.

At the top, this peak was considerably lower than the adjacent mountain, and slightly lower than the jagged peaks of the next range across the narrow valley behind it. To Roscoe, it seemed more intimidating now, with an element of eeriness that he had not noticed the first time.

Clay turned his back against the brisk north wind and scanned the surroundings. To him, nothing had changed. "How should we begin?" he said to no one in particular. He retrieved the map from his coat pocket, unfolded it on the ground and weighted it down with rocks on all edges to keep the wind from whisking it away. Then out came the medallion. He placed it on the map with the center hole precisely at the point where they were, rotating it to different positions, and periodically surveying the surroundings. Carlos and Roscoe knelt beside him, closely scrutinizing every possibility. Now and then, Clay would stand up, pace around the plateau, and then he'd go back to studying the map, searching for some tiny detail that they might have overlooked.

Roscoe's knees were sore from kneeling on the rocks. He stood, stepped over to the lopsided granite pedestal and leaned against it. Feelings of discouragement crept in. *Nothing different from the first time,* he thought. He considered trying to convince Clay that this might be a waste of time, and that they should just go back to Yuma and get on a train... going anywhere. He could see the determination slowly draining from Clay, too.

Then, suddenly, Carlos suggested a fresh, new idea; he had been pondering the possibility for a while. "What if the medallion is *not* a *part* of the map?"

"What d'y'all mean?" Clay said. "Of course, it's part of the map. That's why Victor Flores made it and scribed "llave" on this peak. It only means that the medallion—the key—is part of the map."

"That's true," Carlos responded. "But... maybe it's not a part of the paper map... but a map all its own." He pointed to the silver coin. "May I hold it, please?"

Clay plucked the medallion from the map and handed it to Carlos. He wasn't sure where Carlos was going with this idea, but it was certainly worth hearing him out.

Roscoe just stood, leaning against the rock pedestal, unconsciously brushing his hand across the top surface, removing the sand and dirt that had collected on it over time.

Carlos examined the medallion, and then gazed at the nearby mountain peaks on the very close horizons, turning several times to see them all. His eyes went back and forth from the peaks to the medallion. On the third pass of scanning the peaks, he stopped facing the eastern range across the valley, held the medallion up, comparing.

"What do y'all see?" Clay inquired.

"Look at this," Carlos said. "The peaks on those mountains over there..."

Clay and Roscoe both directed their attention to the peaks where Carlos pointed.

"The holes in the medallion are the same shape and position as those peaks over there." He held the medallion higher, aligning the holes in the coin with the mountain peaks. They seemed to be a very close match. "Here... look for yourself." Carlos offered the coin to Clay.

"Sure enough," Clay said as he held the medallion against the mountain peak horizon. "They match almost perfectly." He lowered the silver disc and stared at Carlos. "What do y'all think that means?"

"Probably... that small hole in the center shows the location of the gold."

Roscoe studied the mountains across the valley, all the while his fingers rubbing across the top surface of the granite. Those mountains had nearly vertical walls, impossible for the average person to climb... unless there was another way up that wasn't visible from this vantage point. He recalled the medallion and the position of the center hole; if Carlos was right, that would put the gold somewhere on the sheer wall of the mountain. It didn't seem quite plausible.

Clay held the medallion up once more, lining it up with the peaks, and then put an eye up close attempting to look through the center hole. He saw nothing but rock, and he couldn't hold it steady enough to zero in on any one spot.

Carlos tried it. Same results.

"Hey... Clay... Carlos... come look at this," Roscoe said. While unconsciously brushing away the sand from the top of the granite pedestal, his fingers had felt something there that finally registered. A groove, straight and narrow, about two inches long. With his pocket knife, he dug away the sand deeper in the groove to reveal a curved bottom, shaped as if a silver dollar would fit into it.

Curiously, Clay and Carlos examined the groove; Carlos was still holding the medallion, so he had the honor of trying to insert it into the groove. It fit snugly. With a little adjusting, the holes aligned with the mountain peaks. He tilted his head and peered through the center hole. After a few moments, he raised up, grinning as if he had just opened the best Christmas present in his entire life. "It's there," he said calmly and quietly. "If you want to hide something for safekeeping... hide it in the desert."

Clay stooped down to look. There, on a ledge halfway up the vertical mountain face, distinctly sat a square, black box. It was too far away to see much detail, but it could only be one thing—the strongbox containing three hundred pounds of gold bars. Clay was speechless.

Roscoe took his turn to look, and he, too, was at a loss for words. They had, indeed, located the stolen gold that had been missing for nearly two decades.

22

There were no whoops or hollers; no yells or shouts of joy. The three just stood there at the pedestal, facing the mountain range to the east, quietly celebrating their victory. A chilly north wind didn't bother them anymore. The thought of actually finding the gold was certainly satisfying. But now, their next challenge was how to get to it. Nearly twenty years before, four men on foot had put it there, somehow, so there must be a way to get it down from that treacherous looking spot. Even Carlos didn't know of a way up to the ledge. The four bandits were all dead now, and plainly they were the only ones who did. But there didn't seem to be any rush; that box had been hidden in plain sight for almost two decades, and it wasn't likely that anyone else would find it anytime soon.

For several minutes, the ecstasy occupied their thoughts, and then it was bluntly disrupted.

"So... you found the gold," came a startling voice sharply from behind them. Clay knew that distinct voice. Irish accent. Man in the brown suit.

Roscoe and Carlos had never heard the man speak, so the voice was new to them. They turned quickly, instinctively, to see who had so deviously penetrated their secrecy.

With his back still toward the source of the voice, Clay discreetly snatched the medallion from the groove and clenched it in his fist, hopeful that whoever was behind him hadn't seen its position on the pedestal. As he slowly turned around to face the aggressor, he slid it into his trouser pocket. Like Roscoe and Carlos had already seen, not only the man in the brown suit stood before them, but three other men as well, their attire more fitting to cowboys—scuffed boots, dirty, worn blue jeans, dark plaid wool shirts, red bandannas around their necks, battered, black hats covering greasy long hair. All able-bodied men. Under the cover of wind noise, they had managed to approach the plateau without being noticed; the element of surprise had worked in their favor.

Clay, Roscoe, and Carlos all knew this wasn't a social visit. Clay gave a brief thought to drawing his .45 but just as quickly, he abandoned the idea; there were four of them, all armed with similar weapons, and by the appearance of the three ruffians standing at either side of Mr. Brown Suit, they probably knew how to use them, and quite proficiently. It wasn't time to take that chance.

"Where's your fourth man?" Clay said, stalling, assessing the situation.

The man smiled. "He was detained in town due to a slight injury."

"We've met before," Clay said. "But we've never been formally introduced. I'm Clay Edwards." He tipped his bowler hat and gestured to his friends. "This is Roscoe Connor, and on my left is Carlos Volero." Then, without hesitation, he added a bit of sarcastic politeness. "I don't believe I've had the pleasure of hearing your name."

The man sneered. His eyes were searching them for weapons. When he felt certain that Clay was the only one with a sidearm, he, too, tipped his brown pork pie hat and gave a gracious little bow. "Thaddeus Belmont... at your service."

Roscoe's eyes widened and his jaw dropped.

Clay, too, was a bit surprised to learn the man's name, but he retained his poker face.

As he straightened up from the bow, Belmont's right hand went to the revolver on his hip. The gun was quickly trained on Clay, and the other three henchmen drew their six-shooters as well.

"Now, Mr. Edwards," Belmont said calmly. "Drop that forty-five on the ground, and then give me the map and the medallion." He looked directly at Roscoe and then Carlos. "And you two... keep your hands up where I can see them.

Carlos and Roscoe side-stepped, spreading out, holding their hands up about shoulder high as Clay slowly withdrew his gun from the holster and held it off to his side with the barrel pointing toward himself. He knew he could not possibly out-maneuver four guns without jeopardizing his life, as well as Roscoe and Carlos. His every move was sluggish and deliberate, giving him time to think. Carefully, he laid the pistol on the ground, then, in the same slow motion, arose.

"Now the map and the medallion," Belmont ordered.

Clay stepped forward, the toes of his boots at the edge of the map spread on the rocks. "This map?" he said, sounding a bit naive, pointing.

"That map," Belmont snarled.

In the short time he had to think, it occurred to Clay that the map had outlived its usefulness, but Thaddeus Belmont would not get it, regardless of its lack in value. He gently removed the stones pinning it down, and holding it at one corner, he raised up with the parchment violently waving, twisting in the wind. Making it appear accidental, he released his grip. The map soared high into the air as if it had wings, tumbling and rolling.

For a moment, Clay thought Belmont would leap into the air in a feeble attempt to catch the flying parchment, giving him the opportunity to get the drop on Belmont. But Belmont didn't move, and within a few seconds, the map was out of sight beyond the mountain peaks—gone forever, thanks to the gusty north zephyr. The other three men helplessly watched the map float out of sight.

Nice trick, Carlos thought.

With anger in his eyes, Belmont looked at Clay. "You did that on purpose—"

"No... it was an accident. Honest." Clay held his hands out to his sides; he raised his right arm from the elbow, and dropped it again.

"Well, no big loss," Belmont said, like he was trying to convince Clay that he wasn't concerned. "I know the medallion is the important part. Let's have it."

"I'm curious," Clay said. "How did y'all know about the medallion?"

Carlos made eye contact with Roscoe. He was almost certain that Clay's right arm movement had been a signal. He also knew that both Clay and Roscoe were still armed, their well-concealed derringers ready at moment's notice. Now, Clay was making small talk with Belmont, buying time, and he was certainly watching for the right opportunity. Roscoe had seen it, too. He thought it had been Clay's way of telling him to get ready. He made a similar gesture with his right arm that Carlos could see.

Thaddeus Belmont glared at Clay a few seconds, and then he spoke: "I know about the medallion because it was supposed to be given to me after Victor Flores made it."

"But... why?" Clay asked.

"That's none of your business, Clay Edwards. Now... give me the medallion."

Carlos could clearly see that Belmont was losing his patience. His three backup men were getting restless. He was quite sure that Clay was waiting for that right moment—a distraction that would allow him to catch Belmont off-guard. Between Clay and Roscoe, they had four shots without reloading the double-barrel derringers. Four shots. Four targets. Close range. Not much time.

An idea came to him. It had worked once before and it could work again.

Clay was aware that Belmont wasn't backing down; he had only one last bargaining chip left—the silver medallion—and he would have to make this one count. He slid his fingers down into his trouser pocket and pulled out the shiny, silver disc, allowing Belmont to see it was there in his hand. "Is this what you want?" he asked.

Belmont eyed the silver piece in Clay's hand. "Yes," he said in a disgusting tone. "Now, toss it here."

Clay looked down at his left hand holding the silver. He

glanced back at Carlos, and then Roscoe. He looked at Belmont, judging the distance, the wind. His left hand rose quickly, his thumb flipping the coin from his grasp. It sailed into the air, spinning, glittering in the sunlight, over Belmont's outstretched hand, past the three gunmen, over the cliff into oblivion.

This was the moment Carlos had been waiting for; in his loudest possible voice he shouted "DON'T SHOOT THE PIANO PLAYER!" He closed his eyes in fear of what might happen next.

The shout was such an alarming distraction that Belmont and his three men threw their attention at Carlos long enough for Clay and Roscoe to jerk the derringers into action and to each fire twice, all four slugs hitting their targets. Belmont's pistol flew out of his hand, as his forearm turned red with blood. He fell to his knees.

When Carlos heard the four shots, and then no more, he opened his eyes to see one of the henchmen sprawled out flat on his back, motionless, blood spurting from his shoulder, while the other two rolled on the ground, screaming in pain, each with a pant leg soaked in red. None of them had gotten off a single shot.

Roscoe was reloading.

Clay picked up his revolver. "Thanks, Carlos... good shot, Roscoe," he called out. He stepped over to where Belmont sat on the ground, clutching his wounded arm, his gun out of reach. "Now," Clay said in a stern voice, pointing his gun at Belmont's face. "Maybe y'all would like to try again... tell me how y'all knew about the medallion?"

Belmont glanced around in a daze at his fallen comrades, wondering how they had been so quickly defeated, and then looked up at Clay and the .45 staring down at him. "The Wells Fargo agent was a good friend; he told me when and where the gold shipments were going. I told the boys, and they hit this good one. But then they all got killed... except for Victor, and while he was in prison, I told him to make me a map. And I guess you know all the rest."

Roscoe and Carlos had taken the guns from the two outlaws with leg wounds. They hadn't found any weapon by the third man, but he was unconscious. They pitched the guns in a pile with Belmont's, and stood there beside Clay.

Unnoticed, the unconscious man had come to. Belmont saw it, though, and when the downed man raised up on one elbow with his gun in hand, Belmont yelled, "Shoot them, Jake, shoot them."

"I wouldn't do that if I was you," a strong, gravelly voice called out.

23

Just as Belmont had arrived undetected, so did Sheriff Gus Livingston and his deputies. One of the deputies stepped swiftly over to the gunman on the ground, pumped the lever action Winchester rifle that was already pointed at him. The outlaw dropped his pistol and fell back to the ground.

The tall, lanky, gray-haired sheriff saw that Belmont had been disarmed and was bleeding, as well as the other two. With his revolver pointed at Clay he said, "Put the gun down."

Clay dropped his hand holding the weapon to his side, muzzle pointed at the ground, and stepped back about six feet. "Howdy, Sheriff," he said, and then let out a well-deserved sigh, glad that this was over, glad to be standing upright and breathing. "Are we in trouble?"

Sheriff Livingston lowered and holstered his gun. "No... I don't think so." He surveyed the entire area, taking a long look at Clay, and then Roscoe, both still holding their firearms.

His deputies were busy attending to the three moaning outlaws, securing their hands with handcuffs, and tying the outlaws' own kerchiefs around legs and arms as temporary bandages.

When Belmont had been hoisted to his feet by a couple of deputies, Livingston addressed him: "Thaddeus Belmont... you're under arrest for the murder of Vince Carter... and conspiring to rob a stagecoach in eighteen eighty-five." He stepped up closer to Belmont and peered deep into his eyes.

"You can't prove I killed that cowpoke," Belmont snarled.

"Sure I can," said the sheriff. "Four eye witnesses... seen ya do it."

"Well... I didn't rob any stagecoach."

"No, you didn't... but your gang did... and you helped 'em. And if you don't bleed to death before we get you back to town, we're gonna put you in a nice room at the Yuma Prison for a long time."

Clay's thoughts slipped back to his brief acquaintance with Vince Carter; it made him feel good that justice was coming to Vince's killer.

Stunned with the outcome of the day's events, Roscoe and Carlos stood beside Clay and watched the deputies assist the wounded criminals to the trail down the mountain where all the horses awaited.

Livingston turned to them. "I've known Carlos since he was a little boy. But which one of you two fellas is Clay Edwards?" He reached down and took the revolver from Clay's hand.

"That's me," Clay said. "How do y'all know my name?"

"Hotel register... in Castle Dome. They said you was off somewhere with Carlos." The sheriff put Clay's gun up to his nose and sniffed. "This gun ain't been fired," he said.

"No, sir."

"Well, I saw that single shot derringer in your friend's hand..." Livingston looked, but it wasn't there anymore.

"Two shot," Roscoe said. "Double barrel." He shook it loose from his coat sleeve and held it out for the sheriff to examine.

Livingston thought for a moment, recalling quite clearly four bullet wounds. "Now, you didn't do *all* that damage with this."

"No, sir, he didn't," Clay responded. "I did half of it with this one." He produced his derringer that still held two empty shells. "How did you know where to find us?"

"Didn't know. We tracked Belmont out here."

"So, y'all knew he was the fifth member of the gang that robbed the stage?"

"Nope. Didn't know that either. We were tracking a killer."

"But... y'all told him—"

"I heard him tell *you*... and that's as good as a confession in my book."

They discussed the details of the confrontation and why it occurred, and how Carlos was there as their guide.

"So," Sheriff Livingston said. "Did you find the missing gold?"

Roscoe and Clay exchanged glances. Roscoe thought that the answer should come from Clay, and he would agree, whatever the answer.

Clay searched his soul; he certainly wouldn't mind sharing the riches with his two partners, but deep down inside, he knew that wasn't the right thing to do. The gold had been stolen from its rightful owners, and even after all this time, it should be returned. "Yes," he finally said. "We did find it."

A little astonished with the response, the sheriff shook his head. "We've hunted for that gold for years. How'd you do it? Where is it now?"

"With a map we found hidden in a book..."

"Where's the map?" Livingston asked.

"I had to let the wind blow it away, so Belmont didn't get it. But the map wasn't the real reason we found the gold." Clay slid his hand into his trouser pocket and pulled out the medallion. *"This* is what found the strongbox."

Roscoe gasped. "But I saw you throw it over the cliff—"

"What y'all saw me throw over the cliff was a plain old silver dollar. Thaddeus Belmont didn't know the difference, either."

Clay handed the silver medallion to Livingston and walked over to the granite pedestal. "Come over here, Sheriff. We'll show you how to see where the gold is hidden." He waited for the sheriff to step up to the four feet tall rock. "It was actually Carlos who figured it out... so I hope there's a reward in it for him."

They demonstrated the use of the medallion in the groove on the pedestal. "Don't know how y'all will get it down from there."

24

The Colorado River was running low due to lack of rainfall in the north; the steamboats were hung up on sandbars. The best alternative—the only alternative—was the stagecoach back to Yuma from Castle Dome City.

"So," Carlos said, when they were standing on Main Street in Yuma again. "Where will you go next?"

"Haven't decided for sure," Clay replied. "But I'd guess that we'll be on the morning train to somewhere."

"What about you, Carlos?" Roscoe asked. "What's in your

future plans."

Carlos tipped his big hat back on his head, thought a moment. "I think I will go back to Castle Dome... give Lolita Flores another visit." He winked. "I'm older now."

Clay and Roscoe grinned.

"Well, okay," Carlos said. "I have business to attend to now, but I'll see you at the depot tomorrow morning to say good-bye." He shook their hands and walked down the street. He had a gold nugget to sell for cash.

Roscoe turned to Clay. "Where *are* we going? Have you given it any thought?"

"Well," Clay replied. "There's a lot of places we haven't been to..."

"I was reading a magazine article," Roscoe said, "back at the Castle Dome Hotel... Harper's Weekly... 'bout some pirate ships loaded with gold and silver from Mexico... two hundred years ago."

Clay stared at his best friend with his best poker face. "And..."

"The ships sank in a storm in shallow water near the Florida Keys, and the gold's never been found."

Clay pondered the thought a few moments. "Never been to Florida... I've heard it's nice this time of year. Can y'all swim?"

"Not very good."

"Me neither. But I s'pose we could learn."

DON'T SHOOT THE THE PIANO PLAYER

PART TWO

1

"We're lost," one of the deputies insisted. The other three agreed with him.

"We're *not lost*, Dan," said Sheriff Gus Livingston. "Just because we can't find that mountain doesn't necessarily mean that *we* are lost."

"Well, without that map," Dan replied, "I don't think we're gonna find it."

"You might be right," Gus said. "We'll go back to Yuma and find Carlos. Maybe he can help us."

It had been more than two weeks since Sheriff Livingston captured Vince Carter's killer.   More than two weeks since the 1885 gold heist was finally solved. More than two weeks since Clay Edwards and Roscoe Connor boarded the eastbound Southern Pacific at Yuma. But the sheriff had kept the discovery of the missing gold confidential, to avoid another wave of treasure hunters, at least until he had time to recover it. Thaddeus Belmont was beginning a life-sentence in the Yuma Territorial Prison for murder. But he would stand trial for the 1885 stagecoach hold up, as well. Gus Livingston was determined to close that case with a dignified conclusion, so that the proper rewards be distributed to the deserving parties.

The sheriff and four deputies set out for the Castle Dome mining district, prepared to recover the strongbox full of gold bars and return it to Yuma, where it would be used as evidence in the upcoming trial. But the desert and its mountains were foreboding and mysterious, just as always. After two days of searching, they were unable to locate that key mountaintop again; the previous tracks of the first expedition had been erased by wind and rain, and without Victor Flores's map, they might search for months and never find it. So they returned to Yuma empty-handed.

When Carlos Volero returned to Yuma, too, after a visit to Castle Dome City, where he had rekindled some romantic flames with Lolita Flores, he was pleasantly surprised by a telegram from his new friends, Clay and Roscoe. They had spent some time in El Paso, and now they were at a hotel in Del Rio, Texas for a while; they were curious about developments in certain matters. Carlos was about to reply when Sheriff Livingston stopped him on the street.

"Buenos Dias, Carlos," the sheriff greeted him.

"Buenos Dias, Sheriff," Carlos returned.

"By any chance, could you find that mountain again where we captured Belmont? We tried, but..."

Carlos thought a moment. Sheriff Livingston wanted to recover the gold. He suspected the sheriff needed his help, as it would be difficult for anyone to find it, even if they had been there once before. "Well," he replied hesitantly, trying not to sound too eager with his knowledge. "I don't know... maybe."

"I know your Navajo grandfather taught you a lot about the desert," Gus said. "And I know you go to Castle Dome fairly often. And I know that you helped those two dandy fellas find the mountain."

Carlos felt as if he were being backed into a corner. Gus was familiar with his activities, although he was unaware of any details, just like anyone else.

"Now Carlos," the sheriff continued. "I know you come back with gold nuggets every now and then, so I figure you must be doin' some prospecting up in the Castle Dome District, and I figure you must know your way around up there."

"Well, yes, I go there..."

"Would you be willing to help me and my deputies find that mountain again? I'll make it worth your while."

Carlos gazed up and down the street, contemplating his answer. He would have to lead them on a different route, as to not let them get too familiar. "Well, I s'pose I could try to help you, Sheriff."

"Oh... and one other thing," Gus said. "Do you happen to know where those two fellas got off to? The judge says they need to testify in court about what Belmont told them regarding the stage robbery."

"I got a telegram from them this morning," Carlos replied. "Clay and Roscoe are at a hotel in Del Rio, Texas. I was on my way to the telegraph office to send them a reply."

"Well, then... tell them that Sheriff Livingston requests their return to Yuma... not because they're in trouble, but because I need their help in getting a conviction on Belmont. Oh... and you should mention a possible reward." Gus winked.

Carlos went to the railroad depot telegraph office and sent the message.

At La Hacienda Hotel in Del Rio, there was a knock on the door.

"Who's there?" Clay called out.

"Western Union messenger... telegram for Clay Edwards," was the reply from outside.

Clay opened the door, almost certain that the telegram

must be from Carlos. He signed the receipt and tipped the messenger a silver dollar.

"Thank you," the messenger responded with a smile. "Shall I wait here for your reply?"

"No," Clay said. "Not necessary... I know where your office is."

The messenger left and Clay closed the door, tore open the envelope. Roscoe was immediately at his side, eager to see the response from Carlos. It wasn't exactly what he had expected, but it didn't surprise him. Nor, did it surprise Clay.

"So... the sheriff wants us back in Yuma," Roscoe said.

"Figured as much," Clay replied. "Maybe we'll get some of that gold after all."

"Funny," Roscoe added. "Carlos doesn't say if he saw Lolita Flores again."

"S'pose if we want to find out, we'd better go back to Yuma."

Roscoe didn't object. "I was beginning to like it there, anyway."

Clay wrote the reply message on the back of the paper: *Will arrive Yuma depot three days. Please reserve room at Vendome. Clay. Roscoe.* "I'll take this to the telegraph office... I'll meet y'all at the cafe for supper."

2

Livingston didn't want to wait for Clay and Roscoe to return; the strongbox had to be recovered as soon as possible. He told Carlos to make the hotel reservation and leave a message with the clerk, in case the undertaking lasted longer than three days. When Carlos had completed the task, Gus had a horse all saddled and outfitted, waiting for him. It was still early in the day; on horseback, they could make it to the mountains by nightfall.

Just as he had planned, Carlos made sure that the route to the key mountain completely differed from how the sheriff and his deputies had gotten there before from Castle Dome City. He included a few extra turns, weaving through the mountains to keep adding as much confusion as possible. After camping for one night, they arrived at the base of the sheer rock wall where the strongbox perched on a ledge high above them. Carlos purposely kept them away from the trail leading to the key peak, and out of sight range from the petroglyph bird etched on the adjacent mountain wall.

He pointed upward. "The strongbox is on that ledge."

"Are you sure this is it?" Livingston asked.

"Yes, I'm sure." Carlos pointed to the opposite low peak. "That's the point where you looked through the hole in the medallion."

Livingston peered up at the low peak. He could see the pedestal rock as he remembered. "Okay... now we have to figure out how to get up to that ledge."

"I'll scout for a way up there," Carlos volunteered. "Those robbers must've found a way... so can I."

"Very well," Gus replied. "We'll wait here."

Carlos left his horse with the others and started out on foot. He already knew where the path was, but he had to convince the sheriff this was a mission of discovery. The way up to the narrow ledge was an easy climb on rocks that were arranged almost like a staircase. At the top, the strongbox lay about a hundred feet away along the ledge that varied in width, some portions only a foot, but passable with care. Carlos slowly made his way to the box, then called down to the sheriff and deputies. "Here it is, Sheriff." He knelt down next to it and brushed away the layer of dust from the lid, revealing the Wells Fargo name engraved in the metal. "It says Wells Fargo on the top... and the lock is broken."

"Okay," Gus yelled. "Can you open it?"

With his hunting knife, Carlos pried at the edge of the lid until there was a gap large enough to slip his hand in. The rusted hinges squealed as the top raised. Shiny gold bars glistened in the sun. "There's gold, alright," he called out.

"Okay," Gus said. "How do I get up there?"

"Around the corner from you... you'll see the steps in the rocks... it's an easy climb. But be careful on the ledge... some parts are quite narrow."

Gus followed the directions. It took him a little longer to reach the ledge as he wasn't quite as agile as young Carlos. When he saw the strongbox, two feet square and a foot high, he nearly came to tears. It was a beautiful sight. He reached down and pulled out one of the ten-pound bars, turning it over several times, examining it, convincing himself that it was real. After a few moments, he shouted down to his deputies. "Dan. Bring some ropes and gloves up here. We'll lower it down... too dangerous to carry it down those rocks."

Dan brought up the ropes and leather gloves. They tied a rope to each handle on the sides of the box, then carefully slid it to the edge.

Gus and Dan were both big, strong men, but Carlos made a suggestion with their best interest in mind. "Why don't you take out half of the bars. Then bring the box up again and lower the rest. It might be easier."

Without even considering the proposal, Gus said, "I think we can do it this way." He and Dan pulled on the leather gloves and gripped the ropes firmly. Dan gave the box a push with his foot. It teetered on the edge of the cliff, and then dropped about two feet, nearly causing Dan to lose his footing. As they lowered the box down, the weight seemed to increase, and fifty feet from the bottom, they couldn't hold it any more. It went crashing down to the ground. The box remained in tact, however, the lid flew open and the gold bars scattered about like cord wood in a heap.

Gus looked at Carlos, who was trying his best to hide a foolish grin.

"I... I..." Carlos stuttered.

"Never mind," said Gus, disgusted with himself, mostly, for not listening to Carlos's advice.

By the time Gus, Dan, and Carlos climbed back down, the other deputies had picked up the gold bars and had them packed in the canvas slings that draped over the back of the extra pack mule. The empty box hung on one side. They were ready to start the long journey back to Yuma.

3

With the gold ingots still in the canvas slings safely secured in one of his locked jail cells late that night, Sheriff Livingston and the four deputies retired for some much-needed rest. The overnight jailer could keep a close eye on the gold.

Carlos wasted no time getting to his hogan at the edge of town, and fell into his bed. It had been a long, grueling day.

Early the next morning, Livingston and the deputies reunited at the jail. The gold needed to be packed back in the strongbox and transferred to the bank's vault where it would be more secure. So far, the public was unaware of the recovery, and Gus wanted to keep it that way for a while. He had made arrangements with the bank president to enter through a back door, where they would unload the strongbox from a shrouded wagon.

As the deputies removed the gold bars from the canvas slings and stacked them neatly in the box, Gus looked on with a strong sense of satisfaction. But suddenly, something didn't seem quite right. "Hold up a minute," he told the men. "How many bars did you put into the strongbox?"

"Didn't count 'em, Gus," Dan replied.

"Well, take them out again and count."

Twenty bars were all laid out on the jail cell floor.

"Is that it?" Gus said. "Are you sure there aren't any more left in the canvas?"

"That's all of them," Dan said as he shook the canvas slings, confirming that none were there.

"There should be thirty bars—ten pounds each—three hundred pounds."

"Well, Gus... you were there when we took it off that ledge... and when we packed it up to haul," Dan said. "You were with us the whole time. Can't imagine how we could've missed ten bars."

"Well, if my memory ain't failing me, I could swear that it was s'posed to be thirty bars, three hundred pounds."

They recounted three times. Twenty bars.

"I'll have the Wells Fargo agent dig out the records," Gus said. "They should have documents to verify the amount of gold that should've been in that shipment. In the meantime, guard this gold with your lives until I get back, and then we'll get it to the bank vault."

At the Wells Fargo office, Agent Abraham Sims greeted the sheriff from behind his desk. "G'mornin' Gus," he said with a cordial smile. "What can I do for you?"

"Mornin' Abe. I'd like for you to look up some old records."

"Would this have anything to do with that old stage

robbery? There's been a lot of talk going around about that lately."

"Yeah," Gus replied. "January twelfth, eighteen eighty-five. Can ya dig 'em out for me?"

"What d'ya need to know?" Sims asked.

"The details of that gold shipment..."

"Okay, I'll see what I can find." Sims went to the back of the room where dozens of large ledger books lined the shelves like a library. He ran his forefinger across the spines of the books, searching the dates scribed on them. "Let's see... it should be here somewhere... AH! Here it is... January, eighteen eighty-five." Abe pulled the two inches thick ten-by-twelve inch volume off the shelf and laid it on the table. He flipped open the green-colored hard cover and began thumbing through the pages, looking at the dates. By then, Gus was at his side, eyeing the hand-written data filling each page, showing trip dates, passenger lists, cargo details, departure times, mid-route stops, destination arrivals, driver names... everything pertaining to the trip. Gus was confident he would find the information he needed.

But among the pages for January twelfth that detailed arrivals and departures in Yuma, Ehrenberg, La Paz, Tyson Wells, Castle Dome City... everywhere in the region where there was—or had been—a Wells Fargo terminal, there was no record of a gold shipment of this size. Smaller ones were listed, but they all had reached their intended destinations without incident. The page listing details about the coach that had been robbed somewhere between Tyson Wells and Yuma, carrying three hundred pounds of gold was missing; apparently it had been removed from the book.

"What do you know about this?" Gus asked in a demanding tone.

Abe Sims just shrugged his shoulders; a scared, puzzled

expression filled his face. "I... I... don't... know..."

"Who was the agent here at that time?"

"I... I... don't know... I have no way of knowing that."

"What do you know about big gold shipments? Are they all handled this way? With no record?"

"No, Gus, they aren't. Here, look at these others." Abe pointed out other smaller shipments on other stages. "The gold bullion in bars are all stamped with the mine and smelter name where they came from... and a number... those are always recorded in our trip records."

Livingston studied the data for other shipments, some as large as fifty or a hundred pounds; all the recorded information coincided with what Abe had said. "Then, why ain't there no record of the January twelfth trip that got held up?"

"I don't know... shipments of that size don't usually have passengers aboard... so naturally, there wouldn't be a passenger list. If you had a mine or smelter name from one of the bars, maybe they would have some record."

"You say *all* the bars are stamped?" Gus said.

"Yes... on the bottom of each bar," Sims replied. "But as long as that gold hasn't been found, it'll be pretty difficult to know which smelter it came from."

Gus inspected the book closely; it appeared that a page had been torn out. It didn't seem likely that any more could be learned from these records.

"Okay, Abe. You've been helpful. Thanks."

Gus hurried back to the jail. Deputies Dan and Albert were waiting for him, sitting on either side of the strongbox with loaded Winchester rifles laid across their knees.

"So, did ya find out?" Dan asked.

"No," Gus replied. "The records for that shipment have

been removed, and Abe Sims knows nothing about it. But he did give me one bit of information." Gus pried open the strongbox and hoisted one of the gold bars up onto the table. "The mines and smelters stamp the bars to identify them." He turned it over, exposing the bottom side. There was no identifying stamp. He lifted another bar out of the box. Nothing on that one, either. One by one, they checked all the bars; they were all blank.

With no identifying stamps, and with no record of where this gold shipment originated or where it was destined, the sheriff's job had become more difficult than he had anticipated. And the lack of identity or documents also meant that no one—individual or business concern—could lay claim to that gold.

But Sheriff Gus Livingston was still certain that he remembered *three hundred pounds of gold* had been stolen from that stagecoach. He was just a young deputy at the time; it was a long time ago; but his memory couldn't be that rusty. There were ten bars missing. He was sure of it. Period.

The only survivor of the gang after the hold up—besides Thaddeus Belmont—was Victor Flores. He had been closely watched after he was released from prison, and even if he had managed to go back out to the mountain, undetected, to make the map and the medallion, as Clay Edwards had claimed at the time of Belmont's arrest, he would not have gotten the gold from the box, considering his poor health and limited physical capability. It just didn't seem possible. Now he was dead.

Thaddeus Belmont was in search of the gold, desperately trying to acquire the medallion—the key to the map. He didn't know the gold's location. His three accomplices weren't in any condition to get to it after Clay and Roscoe severely wounded them.

That left Clay Edwards and Roscoe Connor to be the only other persons to know about the strongbox sitting on that ledge. They had given Gus the medallion, assuring him that they thought the gold should be returned to its rightful owners. And Gus had watched them board the eastbound Southern Pacific train car the day following Belmont's arrest. They'd had no possible means.

Apparently, there were more people involved in the stagecoach heist. Someone at the smelter left the gold bars blank, without the identifying stamps, making them impossible to trace. Many of the mines and smelters of those days had since closed when the ore was depleted. Someone at Wells Fargo either omitted or removed the conveyance records. No records. No driver name. No passengers. No one to testify.

With or without the missing ten bars of gold, Gus Livingston was determined to put Thaddeus Belmont on trial for stagecoach robbery.

"Sheriff! Sheriff!" another deputy shouted, rushing through the door, nearly out of breath. "Thaddeus Belmont has escaped from the Yuma Prison!"

4

Even at a distance, there was no mistaking Carlos in his blue shirt, colorful serape, and wide-brimmed straw hat that allowed just a little of his onyx black hair to show. His broad smile beamed with sincere friendship as he raised his hand in a welcoming wave. Carlos Volero was truly a gem of the Arizona desert; Roscoe and Clay were genuinely happy to see him again. As they waited for their four satchels to be unloaded from the baggage car, they noticed that, as usual, the sun was shining in Yuma; although it was still only early in February, even at just 9:30 in the morning, it felt warm.

Carlos met them on the platform. "Welcome back," he said as he threw his arms out from under the serape and they all embraced in a friendly hug. "It's so good to see you again."

"We missed y'all, Carlos," Clay admitted.

"We're really glad to see you," Roscoe added.

The baggage cart arrived on the platform; Clay and Roscoe waited for several other passengers to collect their luggage, and then retrieved their satchels.

"Your room at the Vendome Hotel is reserved," Carlos informed them. "And there is a message waiting for you at the desk, but you can disregard it now."

"Message?" Clay asked. "What's the message?"

"I left it for you in case we weren't back yet when you arrived this morning."

"We?" Roscoe was curious. "Where were you?"

"I was gone with Sheriff Gus up to the mountains... didn't know if we'd be back in time, but we got back late last night."

"He was after the gold, I'd bet," Clay said.

"Yes... and on their first try, Gus and the deputies got lost... couldn't find it... so they came back and asked me to go with them."

"So, did y'all find the gold?"

Carlos leaned toward Clay and whispered, "Yeah, I found it. Sheriff wants it kept quiet for now."

"Where is it now?"

"Gus locked it up in a jail cell last night, but I think they were gonna secretly move it to the bank's vault today." Carlos straightened up and in a louder tone he said, "Come... I'll walk with you to the hotel."

"We should stop by the Sheriff's Office and let him know we're here," Clay suggested.

"Okay... it's practically on the way."

5

"How could Belmont—or anybody else—break out of that prison?" Sheriff Livingston growled.

"They've got extra guards out searching the area, but so far, nothing," the deputy replied. "They don't know how he did it... figured it was early this morning when the guards were changing. He must've seen his chance, and he took it."

"Yeah... or maybe he had help," Gus returned.

"He seems to be pretty clever," deputy Dan said.

"He might be clever," Gus replied, "but I don't think he's smart."

"There's a difference?"

"Anyone who shoots another unarmed man in cold blood in broad daylight in front of witnesses... can't be too smart."

Carlos entered the office with a grin wider than Madison Avenue. Clay and Roscoe followed.

"G'mornin', Sheriff," Carlos said. He stared at all the serious frowns around the room, unaware of the latest developments.

Gus managed to squeeze out a smile when he saw Clay and Roscoe; it seemed pleasant, but concern lay just beneath the surface. "Clay Edwards and Roscoe Connor," he said, greeting them with a friendly, firm handshake. "Wasn't sure if you'd be willing to come back all the way from Texas."

"Well," Clay replied with a boyish grin. "We didn't like the idea of our faces on a Wanted poster."

Gus let out a slight laugh. "The only face on a Wanted poster now will be Thaddeus Belmont."

Clay and Roscoe both displayed curious, confused expressions. "But... he's already locked up in prison," Roscoe said.

"He *was* in prison," Gus said, quite discouraged. "We just got word that he escaped this morning."

"Escaped!" Carlos exclaimed. "You mean... he's gone?"

"Yep... gone," Gus replied. "I figure he had help, though."

"The hombres we wounded up on the mountain?" Clay said.

"Maybe, but doubtful," Gus said. "Doc Hull fixed 'em up, but Jake damn near died by the time we got to Castle Dome, and the other two can hardly walk. My guess is his brother... the fella that Carlos shot in the leg with an arrow."

"That's Belmont's brother?" Carlos asked, his eyes wide with astonishment.

"Yeah... Jules... Thaddeus Belmont's brother."

"So they're prob'ly long gone from the Territory by now," Clay said.

"I don't think so," Gus said. "Belmont wants that gold... but he'll lay low for a while."

"Except... you already have the gold," Carlos said, nodding toward the strongbox on the floor.

"Belmont doesn't know that... nobody knows that except the people in this room."

"But he knows that we located the strongbox, and that Clay and Roscoe want it, too..."

The sheriff held up his hand as a signal for Carlos to stop. "All Belmont knows is that Clay and Roscoe got on a train and left... without the gold."

"But how...?"

"I told him... that's how... and I also led him to believe that Clay and Roscoe did *not* show me or tell me where it is. I did that in hopes that I could use that as a way to put the rest of his gang behind bars... when they all recover from the wounds the three of you inflicted, and they try to get the gold. So I believe he and his brother are probably still in the Territory...

hiding out... and they'll wait for the right opportunity."

"But..." Clay said. "There's nothing there for them to get."

Gus thought a moment. "Did Belmont actually see where the strongbox was on that ledge?"

"Don't think so," Clay replied. "He must've heard us talking about it... and he saw us looking in the general direction when they managed to get the jump on us."

"And he thinks you tossed the medallion over the cliff?"

"Yeah."

"Well, they might go looking for that."

"Or... if Belmont *did see,* or if he figured out the general area where we were looking..."

"You're right, young man," Gus said. He thought some more. "That's exactly why we'll hafta put the strongbox back where it was."

"You want to put the gold back up on that ledge?" Deputy Dan argued.

"Not the gold," Gus replied. "Just the empty box."

Dan wasn't sure the plan would work. "If they see any of us goin' back out there... and you can be sure they'll be watching... they'll figure out that we're settin' a trap."

Carlos jumped into the conversation: "I know how we can get it there... so they'll never suspect."

"What's your idea?" the sheriff asked.

"Fred... from Tyson Wells."

Gus looked curiously at Carlos. "Who is Fred?"

"Fred Kuehn... he hauls freight with a wagon and four mules... from Yuma to all around the mining districts and Tyson Wells... and it's about time for him to be here again for another load."

"How d'ya know him?"

"I've ridden with him several times... he's Mike Wells' nephew."

"Can he be trusted?"

"Yeah... he's a good fella."

After contemplating the suggestion from Carlos, the sheriff came to a conclusion. "Okay," he said. "Get the word out around town that we couldn't find the gold... that it's still out there."

6

Clay and Roscoe checked into the Vendome Hotel; they had been relaxing all day on the train, but with the new turn of events, they needed something cold from the Ruby Saloon to calm their nerves.

"Will y'all join us for a cold beer?" Clay asked Carlos.

"Sure."

Jack Dunne, the bartender and owner of the hotel, remembered Clay and Roscoe from their stay here more than a month ago. "Good to see you fellas again."

"Good to see y'all again, too, Jack"

"So did you fellas find that mountain you were looking for?"

Clay took off his hat and set it on the bar. He thought Jack was one of the most friendly people he'd met in Yuma, other than Carlos, but the sheriff had warned them about spilling any information to *anyone.* "Oh... we spent two or three weeks up in Castle Dome, but we didn't find what we went for," he said. "But we had a good time." He tossed a half-dollar on the bar for the three five-cent beers. "Keep the change, Jack... we might have another round later."

They sat at a table across the room where they could talk more privately.

"So, Carlos," Roscoe said. "Did you go back to see Lolita?" He winked and sipped his beer.

Carlos smiled. There wasn't anything to hide about his relationship with Lolita Flores from his good friends. "Yes, a few days after you left on the train, I went to see her."

"So, did you stay the night?" Roscoe winked again.

"Yes, I stayed the night. We talked a lot about the past... and about now."

"You just talked?"

"Well, we needed some time to get to know each other better," Carlos replied. "She knew that was the reason I was there, and perhaps some day we can make a life together... but not right now."

"And the age difference doesn't bother her?"

"She likes me... and I like Lolita... that's what's matters."

"Y'all will be there again real soon," Clay said.

"Yeah, I'll ride to Castle Dome with Fred. Tomorrow he will be loading all his freight, and then we'll leave here Thursday morning."

"Y'all have done this before."

"Yes... that's why it won't appear anything out of the ordinary when we take the strongbox to Castle Dome. I'll wrap it with a blanket and take it out to the mountain with a pack mule."

"We should help you," Roscoe said. "That box must be heavy... hard for one person to get it up on that ledge."

"But you'll have to take the stage from here."

"We can do that."

7

Young Fred Kuehn arrived with his four mules and wagon on Wednesday, just as he always did. His load of goods usually was waiting for him at the railroad depot and the boat docks, but sometimes there were special request items to be picked up at the lumber yard or hardware store. This time, though, another piece of freight awaited him at the back door of the Sheriff's Office. No one knew about it except Carlos.

"Hi, Fred!" Carlos greeted him at the depot freight platform.

"Mi amigo, Carlos," Fred called out joyfully. He was happy to see his friend. When the wagon stopped beside the platform, Carlos was right there to shake his hand.

"Will you ride with me this trip?" Fred inquired.

"Yes," Carlos replied. "I'll be going with you to Castle Dome..." And then he lowered his voice to nearly a whisper. "The sheriff has a box to take there... and I have to go with it."

"What is it?" Fred asked.

"An empty Wells Fargo strongbox."

"Why didn't he put it on the stage?"

"'Cause no one can know about it except us."

"What's the big secret?" Fred was curious.

"I'll tell you about it on the way to Castle Dome."

They were well past the Gila River crossing when the stagecoach bound for Castle Dome caught up with them. Fred was hauling a heavy load, and six horses were faster than four mules. "Hey Freddy... headed for Tyson Wells?" the stage driver called out as he pulled up beside the freight wagon, slowly inching by.

"Yeah, John..." Fred called back. "Got some deliveries in Castle Dome and Stone Cabin first, though."

"Okay," John said. "Have a good trip. And watch the sky... could be some rain coming."

"Thanks, John."

As the coach passed, Clay leaned out the open window and waved. "See y'all in Castle Dome."

At six o'clock, the stagecoach arrived at the Castle Dome Hotel. Clay and Roscoe were the only passengers getting off there; all the others were going on over the pass to the mines.

As the driver tossed down their satchels, Clay asked, "How long d'y'all think it'll take that freight wagon to get here?"

"The one we passed back at the Gila River?"

"Yeah... that one."

"Oh, I'd say Fred 'll get here in a couple more hours."

"Okay, thanks." Clay joined Roscoe on the boardwalk; they watched as the driver and a stableman hooked up a fresh team of horses to the coach. "Let's go in and get a room," Roscoe said. It was that time of day when the saloon and gambling hall were busy... miners getting off work after a long day.

"D'ya s'pose Carlos will stay with us tonight?" Roscoe asked as they climbed the stairs to the room.

"Hard to say," Clay replied. "He might have other arrangements."

Halfway down the hall, Clay stopped abruptly, staring unbelieving at the cowboy closing his room door and locking it. It didn't seem possible.

Roscoe saw Clay's shocked expression. "What's wrong, Clay?" he asked.

Clay was speechless.

The cowboy turned and started walking toward them, his boot heels making that distinctive sound on the wood floor. He looked up at Clay, tipped his hat back on his head.

Clay couldn't believe his eyes. "Either... y'all are a ghost... or... I'm dreaming... or... Vince Carter has a twin brother."

8

The cowboy looked at Clay, puzzled at first, and then he grinned when he recognized the face and the bowler hat. He thrust his right hand toward Clay. "Sorry I don't remember your name, my friend, but I remember the face."

"I'm Clay Edwards," Clay said, still in a daze with the sight of Vince Carter standing there... alive... and shaking his hand.

"That's right," Vince said. "The gambler fella... we talked down in the saloon a while back."

"Yeah... but..."

"You thought I was dead."

"Yeah."

"Well, my friend, I can assure you that you are *not* shaking hands with a ghost... I *am* quite alive." Vince then offered his hand to Roscoe.

"I'm Roscoe Connor... pleased to meet you."

"I don't believe it!" Clay said. "I'm so glad to see y'all alive and well... but... I guess... I don't quite understand."

"Well," Vince said. "Put your bags in your room, and let's go downstairs and get some grub... I'm starved. I'll try to clear things up for ya."

They found a table in the busy, noisy dining room; the piano accompanied the sounds of clinking glasses and chatter from fifty different voices all talking at once. A bar maid appeared. "Howdy, Vince." She winked at the cowboy. "Special tonight, fellas, is boiled potatoes with chicken 'n gravy."

"Sounds good t' me," said Vince.

"Me too," Clay said.

"Make it three," Roscoe added. "And three beers, too, please."

"Okay, fellas... I'll bring the beers right away... food will be a few minutes." She disappeared in the crowd, headed in the general direction of the bar.

"So," Clay said. "What happened? We were just coming back from Tyson Wells on the stage, and I saw men carrying a casket out of the church, and the desk clerk said it was y'all."

"Yeah," Vince replied. "I guess everybody thought that at first. Ya see, I wasn't even in town that day. Whoever that cowboy was, must've looked kinda like me, and dressed like me... witnesses said that bastard shot him three times at close range in the face... tore him up so bad... nobody could recognize him... and then somebody must've guessed it was me, 'cause I come here a lot bringin' the beef cattle in."

The barmaid set three mugs of beer on the table.

Clay took a gulp. "Do y'all know the shooter?"

"Yeah," Vince replied. "Some fella by the name of Belmont."

"So, do y'all remember the guy at the bar trying to hustle that silver medallion from me?"

Vince eyed Clay. "Yeah, sorta."

"That was Thaddeus Belmont."

Vince was a bit astonished. "No kidding? I gave that fella a bad time. D'ya s'pose he shot that cowpoke, thinkin' it was me... for revenge?"

"Could be," Clay said.

"I heard the Yuma Sheriff caught up with him a couple of weeks after that... got him a life sentence at the Yuma Prison."

"Y'all heard right... but he ain't there anymore."

"What?"

"He broke out... escaped... yesterday morning."

"Are you serious? He's on the loose?"

"Yep," Clay replied. "And the sheriff wants him not only for murdering y'all... but for a stagecoach hold up, too."

"Stagecoach hold up... I didn't hear 'bout any stage hold

up."

"It happened long time ago... eighteen eighty-five. That's why Belmont wanted that silver medallion. It was part of a map... where the gold from the stage robbery was hidden."

"How'd you get it?" Vince asked.

"Me 'n Roscoe found the map and the medallion concealed in an old book, so we thought we'd come out here and try to find the gold."

"If I remember right," Vince said, "you said you're from Mississippi."

Clay nodded.

"And you came all the way out here to Arizona Territory 'cause of a map you found in a book?"

"Well, me 'n Roscoe actually came here from South America—Argentina."

"The map looked pretty authentic," Roscoe added.

"Yeah," Clay agreed. "Turned out... it was."

The barmaid brought three plates of food to the table. She winked at Vince again. "That'll be three dollars and fifteen cents."

Vince dug in his shirt pocket, but Clay held up his hand as if to say "no" to Vince. He reached into his inside coat pocket and produced the money. "Anybody who comes back from the dead," Clay grinned, "deserves a free meal."

"Well, thank you... much obliged," Vince said.

All through the meal, Vince asked questions; Clay and Roscoe supplied answers about how they had discovered the strongbox location, and the chain of events the day Sheriff Livingston arrested Belmont.

"Of course," Roscoe said, "we didn't know at the time that Belmont shot that cowboy until the sheriff informed him that *he was under arrest for the murder of Vince Carter.*"

"Yeah... and now there's a grave with my name on it... but

I'm not in it."

"Any idea who it is?" Clay asked.

"Not a clue... all our cowpokes are accounted for. Could've been just a drifter."

Clay smiled. "I'm just glad it ain't y'all."

9

Twilight had faded into dusk when Carlos and Fred pulled into Castle Dome City. Not usually Fred's nature to stay at the hotel overnight, he decided to enjoy the luxury just this one time, only because Carlos invited. He usually camped along the trail for a few hours each night to give him and the mules a little rest during the long journey. Fred went right to the livery stable to arrange for the mules' accommodations while Carlos arranged for his and Fred's quarters at the hotel. But, unfortunately, there were no available rooms; the desk clerk, however, remembered Carlos's association with Clay and Roscoe. "They checked in earlier—room number seven," he told Carlos. "Their room is big enough."

"Thank you, Andy," Carlos said. He tipped his hat off his head and let it dangle on his back by the chin cord.

"But they're not in the room right now," Andy informed.

"Oh. Well, do you know where they are?"

"They went to the Flora Temple Bar with Vince. They said you'd be arriving, and to let you know."

"Okay... thanks, Andy." Carlos went out the door and circled around to the livery stable. Fred had finished with the mules and was checking his wagon-load of cargo. "So, did you get a room?" he asked.

"The hotel is full... we'll be bunkin' with Clay and Roscoe

tonight."

"We can do that?"

"Sure... but right now, they're over at the Flora Temple... we'll find 'em there."

They heard the honky tonk piano from inside the Flora Temple long before they reached the front entrance. That sound brought back memories to Carlos, but he quickly put them aside. It was likely that Lolita would be there working, and he certainly would be glad to see her again.

Clay, Roscoe, and Vince Carter sat at a table on the far side of the barroom, sipping cold beers. Less crowded than usual, they were easy to spot.

Lolita arrived at the table just about the same time as Carlos; she gave him a little kiss on the cheek. That confirmed she had not lost interest in him; his heart raced just a little.

"Can I get you something?" she asked, her eyes telling more than words could say.

"Two beers," Carlos replied, mesmerized.

Lolita danced away toward the bar.

"Carlos," Clay greeted. "Y'all got the word where we were."

Carlos, still watching Lolita, abruptly directed his attention to Clay. "Yes... how was the stage ride?"

"Same as usual... bumpy."

"The hotel is full," Carlos said as he and Fred sat down in the two empty chairs. "Okay if Fred and me sleep on the floor in your room?"

"No need to sleep on the floor," Roscoe chimed in. "There are two big beds in that room."

Lolita returned with the two foam-topped mugs and set them on the table in front of Carlos. He pushed one in front of Fred.

Fred's eyes widened. "Really?" he said, glancing at Carlos.

"Sure. Just don't tell Angela when you get back to Tyson Wells."

Fred grinned and took a sip of the beer.

Carlos peered across the table at Vince Carter. "You're s'posed to be dead."

Everyone else at the table laughed with amusement. Carlos had not yet learned the good news. But within the next few minutes, he knew the whole story. He was glad that Vince had escaped such a brutal tragedy.

Fred just listened in awe. During the trip from Yuma, Carlos had told him the saga of how Roscoe and Clay had been instrumental in Belmont's arrest, and about Belmont shooting the cowboy; he, too was quite surprised—but happy—that Vince was still alive and well.

Carlos gazed around the room to make sure no one else was paying any attention to the conversation at their table. "Tomorrow, or, maybe the next day I will put the strongbox on a pack mule and take it out to the mountain."

"We'll go with y'all," Clay said.

"Mind if I go, too?" Vince said. "Sounds like you fellas could use some protection."

"Well..." Carlos eyed Vince, not sure if there was really any need for protection. Then he looked at Clay, wondering how much the cowboy knew.

"We explained," Clay said. "An extra gun couldn't hurt."

"I can handle a pistol," Vince said, trying to reassure Carlos. "And y' know... I might have a score to settle with Belmont."

"Do I need to remind all of you?" Carlos argued. "We are not lawmen. We aren't here to hunt Belmont. We are here to put the strongbox back on that ledge... that's all."

"He's right," Roscoe said. "And besides... Belmont is on the run right now. It's very likely that he is in hiding somewhere... and probably not around here."

10

The next morning, Fred wanted to get an early start. Carlos went with him to the livery stable and helped him harness the team. As they unloaded the strongbox from the wagon, Fred asked, "So when are ya taking this thing out to that place?"

"Probably tomorrow," Carlos replied. "I think it might be a waste of time... but it's what the sheriff wants."

"How long will it take?"

"A day out... a day back."

"Want me to haul it out there for ya?"

"No... you'd never make it with the wagon... it's kinda rough country."

"Well, okay... good luck... I'll be seein' ya again." Fred climbed up into the driver seat, took up the reigns and slapped them across the mules' backs. The wagon creaked and groaned under the load, and soon he was gone, on his way to Stone Cabin.

Carlos looked at his pocket watch... it was only 7:00 o'clock. He headed back up to the hotel room to see if the others were awake and ready for breakfast.

Late that afternoon, only two miles from Stone Cabin, Fred noticed two riders on horseback coming from the canyon on his right. They were too far away to know who they might be —probably cowpokes from King Valley Ranch out rounding up cattle. They seemed to be headed for Stone Cabin, maybe to get some supper. But then, they changed direction; their course would intercept Fred's team and wagon on the road up ahead. Fred thought about reaching down to pull out his Winchester rifle he kept hidden with a blanket under the seat.

But the riders were keeping their distance, and so far, they didn't seem to pose any threat.

Suddenly, they cut directly for the road just ahead, picking up speed as they approached closer. Fred still couldn't identify them, but a sinking feeling deep in his gut told him this wasn't a social visit when he saw them pull their bandannas up over their faces, and revolvers out of their holsters. *Road bandits* he thought. But now there wasn't time to get out the rifle, nor would it be a wise move; it could get him shot. "Whoa, Buster... Maggie," he called out to the lead team. They came to a stop just short of where the bandits blocked the road.

"What ya got in the wagon?" one of them shouted, with his six-shooter pointed in Fred's general direction.

Brave and courageous, conditioned to this harsh environment, not much rattled Fred's nerves; he had encountered rattlesnakes, wolves, angry longhorn bulls... just about anything this desert had to offer... but two guns pointed at him by strangers with masks covering their faces was something entirely different. He had no control over the situation as he saw it.

When he didn't answer the bandit's question right away, the masked man shouted again. "I said... what you got in the wagon?"

The voice seemed somewhat familiar to Fred. He took a deep breath. "J-j-just some lumber, and nail kegs... 'n some g-g-general store merchandise."

"Any food in there?" the bandit barked.

"Y-y-yes, mister... take what you want... but please don't shoot me... I'm j-j-just a kid."

The other rider dismounted his horse and walked with a severe limp toward Fred's wagon. "Get down from there," he growled.

Fred climbed down off the seat and stood beside the wagon. When the masked bandit was satisfied that Fred didn't have any weapon, he stepped over to the cargo box, threw back the canvas covering the freight, and began breaking open boxes containing canned goods destined for Bill Scott's General Store at Tyson Wells.

Fred glanced at the other gunman, still on his mount, with a gun pointed at him. There *was* something familiar about him... those eyes... the strange accent... and then it occurred to him; he had hauled supplies and water to a prospector's camp... this man's camp... Belmont's camp. But something inside told him not to give any indication that he knew the man on that horse. It could jeopardize whatever little chance he had of surviving.

The man at the wagon dumped the contents from one of the boxes and began filling it with various canned goods and a big jar of beef jerky. Fred watched him as he carried it to his horse, still favoring his right leg, and then started stuffing the food into the saddle bags. He came back and hoisted a ten-pound sack of flour over the side of the wagon, and carried it to the other horseman, throwing it onto the horse's back. The limp was getting noticeably worse. When he came back that time, he held a length of rope. "Hold out your hands," he told Fred.

Reluctantly, Fred did as he was instructed; the man lashed his wrists together, and then pushed him to the back of the wagon, where he tied his hands to the wagon frame.

"There... by the time you get out that... we'll be long gone." He got back on his horse, and just before the two men rode off, he whipped the two lead mules, sending them off at a trot up the road.

All Fred could do was run along behind the wagon, hoping not to stumble. He glanced off to the side, briefly watching the two bandits riding across the desert to the west. But then it seemed they changed direction and headed back toward Palm Canyon.

With a little luck, Buster and Maggie would go right to the Stone Cabin General Store; they'd done that countless times before.

11

Jonah Yarber saw the four-mule team and wagon coming up the trail toward his store at Stone Cabin, but when he realized there was no driver aboard the wagon, it caused him alarm. Fred was always a bundle of smiles perched on that seat, but today, he wasn't there. Jonah stepped quickly out his doorway and started walking toward the oncoming team, ready to intercept the driver-less rig. He grabbed hold of the bridle of one of the lead mules. "Whoa, Buster," he said. He'd heard Fred call out the mules' names so many times, even he knew them now.

The wagon rattled and creaked to a stop, and then Jonah heard a moaning voice coming from behind it. He hurried to the rear of the wagon, and there, hanging like a side of beef by his tied hands to the wagon frame, Fred's feet were dragging behind. His legs had just given up trying to keep pace with the mules. At one point, he had tried to pull himself up and throw one leg up onto the back of the wagon, but he just couldn't do it. His strength had been drained.

Jonah put his arm around Fred's chest and helped him to stand; Fred was so exhausted that he could barely remain upright.

"What happened?" Jonah cried. "Who did this to you?"

"Two road agents held me up... couple miles back."

Jonah quickly assessed the rope that lashed Fred's hands to

the wagon. "Just hold on, Fred... I'll get a knife."

"I ain't goin' nowhere," Fred moaned.

Half a minute later, Jonah had the rope cut and Fred's hands were free at last.

"Are you hurt?" the storekeeper asked.

"Just my wrists are pretty sore," Fred replied. He pulled his shirt sleeves up; his left wrist was actually bleeding from the rope burns.

"Come on inside," Jonah said. "Let's get that bandaged up."

All the while Jonah was wrapping a strip of white cotton cloth around his wrist, Fred thought about Carlos taking that strongbox out into the mountains. He didn't know *where* Carlos was going exactly, but he'd said tomorrow was *when* he was going. His head was spinning with confusion. Somehow, Carlos had to be warned that Belmont *and* his brother could be headed back to Castle Dome. There would be enough time; he could ride Buster bareback; he'd done that many times.

"I hafta unhitch the team and ride Buster back to Castle Dome," Fred told Jonah. "And I hafta do it tonight. Will it be okay to leave the team and wagon here?"

"Why? You're all tired out," the storekeeper said. "Can't it wait till morning?"

"No... I have to warn Carlos about those men who held me up."

Jonah was a little confused; he thought a moment. "You mean Carlos... that nice young man who's been with you sometimes?"

"Yeah..." Fred explained that Carlos was to return a strongbox into the mountains somewhere as bait for the sheriff to catch Belmont. "But that *must remain a secret... understand?*"

"Sure." It didn't all make sense to Jonah, but he recognized the sincere urgency that Fred was desperately trying to get across. "Belmont is a killer," Fred went on, "and he and his brother have good reason to hold grudges against Carlos."

"I'll look after the team," Jonah assured. "And I'll get my lumber unloaded from the wagon."

"Thanks, Jonah."

"But I hafta tell ya..." Jonah warned. "Buster ain't gonna make it to Tyson Wells without a little rest."

"Oh... I know... he'll get some rest before we go the rest of the way." Fred gazed into Jonah's eyes. "S'pose I could get a bite to eat before I leave?"

Taking only his coat and his trusty Winchester rifle, Fred rode into the night, with only the moon and the stars to guide his way. He hated to punish Buster this way, but he had to keep traveling during the darkness, so Belmont wouldn't see him going back to Castle Dome. It was likely that they would be well off the trail, hiding out, but there wasn't any reason to take any more chances.

By the time Fred was close to Castle Dome City, Buster's pace had long ago slowed from a gait to a walk. He was tired. Fred was tired. They both needed some rest. At 5:00 o'clock in the morning, Fred tied Buster's reigns to a hitching rail beside the Castle Dome Hotel. He could hardly keep his eyes open as he patted the animal's neck. "I owe you one, buddy," he whispered.

Quite doubtful that Carlos and the others were yet awake, Fred decided to just wait downstairs; they would come down for breakfast before heading into the mountains.

An hour later, halfway down the stairs, Roscoe spotted Fred slouched in a chair in the parlor area next to the front desk, fast asleep. He poked Carlos in the ribs. "Isn't that your friend, Fred, over there?"

Carlos peered at the heap of messy, dusty clothes sprawled in the chair, a big, brown hat—Fred's hat—lay on the floor beside the chair, partially covering a lever-action Winchester. He noticed the white bandage on one wrist. Fred certainly looked as if he had been to hell and back. Something was definitely wrong; he couldn't think of any reasonable explanation for Fred's presence here... not now.

The room was already filling with miners coming in for breakfast before their shift. Carlos hurried down the stairs and across the busy dining room to where Fred sat sleeping. He gently shook Fred's shoulder. "Fred... wake up," he said softly.

"He's been here since about five o'clock," Andy the desk clerk said. "And I think that's his mule outside."

Carlos looked out the window to see Buster laying at the hitching rail, head drooped.

He tried, once again, to arouse Fred, but Fred didn't come awake easily. He barely opened his eyes, and in his groggy condition, the sight of Carlos didn't register right away.

"What's wrong?" Carlos asked. "Why are you back here again?"

Fred abruptly opened his eyes wider, his head jerking from side to side, gazing around the room, trying to gain some orientation. He looked at Carlos, and after a long moment he said, "Carlos," and then hoisted himself upright in the chair. He rubbed his eyes and yawned, then stared at the bandage on his wrist, as if it were all foreign to him.

"What happened to you?" Carlos asked.

By then, Roscoe and Clay were there, curiosity getting the better of them.

Fred touched the bandage with the fingers of his right hand, and the burning sensation on both wrists jarred his memory to the frightening events of the previous evening. Sudden consciousness delivered visions and thoughts, still not entirely clear, but at least he remembered what had happened, and why he was here at the Castle Dome Hotel. "Carlos," he said again, and gazed about the room. He saw and recognized Clay and Roscoe, and when he thought there were no others listening, he said softly, "Carlos... Belmont is on his way here."

"What? How do you know that?"

"Two men with masks held me up just before I got to Stone Cabin. It was Belmont and his brother. They tied me to the back of the wagon after one of them stole a bunch of food from my freight. Buster and Maggie know the way to Stone Cabin, 'n I got drug behind the wagon all the way there."

"How do y'all know it was Belmont?" Clay asked.

"I knew that voice... that funny accent..."

"Irish," Clay said, nodding.

"Yeah... and Carlos told me that he shot Belmont's brother in the leg with an arrow... the one fella limped pretty bad."

"Did he know you?" Carlos asked.

"Don't know... I don't think so."

"How do y'all know they're coming here?" Clay questioned.

"First, I saw them heading west, toward the Trigo Mountains and Cibola, but then they turned back toward Palm Canyon... coming this way. I had to come back to warn you."

"Well," Carlos replied. "I think I can speak for all of us... we're mighty grateful for that." He took hold of Fred's arm and urged him to stand. "Now, let's get you upstairs to our room and get you cleaned up a bit."

Clay picked Fred's hat up from the floor; Roscoe grabbed the rifle.

12

Carlos poured water into the wash basin and helped Fred get his dirty shirt and trousers off so he could wash away the dirt and dust that completely covered his whole body from being dragged behind the wagon. Large holes were ripped in his trousers from snagging on sharp rocks.

"He looks about my size," Clay said. "I have a shirt and trousers he can use."

When Fred had dried himself with a towel and donned the clean clothes, he sat in a chair, still tired, but thinking more clearly. "Thanks for the duds," he said to Clay. Not really the kind of clothes he usually wore, he was still grateful.

"Where's the rest of the team... and the wagon?" Carlos asked.

"Still at Stone Cabin... Jonah is looking after them 'til I get back." Then, suddenly a thought occurred to Fred. "Poor Buster is still out at the hitching rail!"

"I'll go take care of him," Roscoe volunteered. "I'll get him over to the livery barn... get him some water and feed."

"Thanks," Fred said. "And I hafta tell the morning stage driver goin' to Tyson Wells to tell Bill at the General Store that I'll be a day late."

"I'll take care of that, too, Roscoe said.

"Okay," Fred replied. "Just *don't tell him why*... okay? I don't want Angela to get all fussed."

Roscoe remembered Angela Scott, and how she fussed over young Fred. "Okay. I'll just tell him you're running behind schedule... not to worry."

After Roscoe left, Fred turned to Carlos and Clay. "You can't go out to wherever it is you're goin' to."

"But we have to get that strongbox back out to the

mountain... Sheriff Gus needs it out there for bait to catch Belmont."

"But what if Belmont is already on his way out there and sees you? You shot his brother in the leg... and Clay shot Belmont in the arm... and all of you helped put him in prison. I don't think he exactly considers any of you his best friends right now."

"He's right about that," Clay said. "But, on the other hand... if the sheriff couldn't find that place again, do y'all think Belmont can?"

Carlos sat in a chair next to Fred, rubbed his chin, thought a moment.

"Remember what Livingston said?" Clay added. "Thaddeus Belmont ain't too smart."

"Yeah..." Carlos admitted. "But maybe his brother, Jules is."

When Roscoe came back a half-hour later, Fred was practically sleeping sitting in the chair. The sound of the door closing startled him back into awareness. Carlos urged him to stand up, and then walked him toward the bed. "You need to lay down for a while... get some rest."

"But... I hafta get goin' back to my freight wagon."

Roscoe had other ideas for Fred. "I think you'd just better stay here for a few hours," he suggested. "Buster is so worn out... I could barely get him to walk over to the livery barn... I think he drank about five gallons of water."

"Poor Buster," Fred cried.

"He needs some rest, too... just like you."

Fred almost fell into the bed. He was asleep before his head hit the pillow.

"Did you get to talk to the stage driver?" Carlos asked.

"Yeah," Roscoe replied. "I told him to tell Bill Scott that Fred might be *two* days late."

13

Three light taps sounded at the door. Roscoe was the closest; he opened it just wide enough to see Vince Carter in the hall.

"Howdy, Roscoe," Vince said.

"Hey, Vince."

"I saw you helpin' the boy in a while ago... is he hurt?"

Roscoe opened the door wider, stepped into the hall. "Not too bad..." he replied quietly. "Fred is just all wore out from ridin' all day and all night, too. He needs to rest."

"I thought he left yesterday morning."

"He did, but he barebacked one of his mules all the way from Stone Cabin during the night."

"Why?"

"He got held up and robbed by Belmont and his brother. So he came back to warn us they're not far away."

Vince peered into the room and saw Fred passed out, sprawled across the bed. "So... what are ya gonna do?"

Carlos overheard the conversation in the hall and came to the doorway. "The plan was to get that strongbox back out to the mountain today... but now, I don't know."

Vince eyed Fred's rifle leaning against the night stand. "Is that Fred's Winchester?"

"Yeah."

"Well, by the looks of things, he won't be needin' it for a while."

"Probably not," Carlos said curiously. "What are you thinking?"

"I'll take the rifle... I'll go with you... that is, if you trust me."

"Of course, I trust you, Vince."

"Okay... Clay and Roscoe can stay here and keep an eye out

for Belmont while you and me go out to put that box wherever you're gonna put it."

Clay joined the others in the hall. "And on horseback," he added, "y'all could prob'ly make it out and back in a day."

Carlos leaned against the door sill, thinking. It was a slim chance that Belmont would ever find his way out to that mountain in one day, and even less chance that he would let himself be seen in Castle Dome City so soon after the prison break. The risk seemed slight. Fred would more than likely sleep all day and half the night. They could be back by the time he woke up; he'd never know his rifle was gone. And getting the strongbox back on that ledge is what Sheriff Livingston wanted him to do.

"I have a horse," Vince said. "We only need one for you... and a pack mule."

"Okay," Carlos said. "We'll leave about noon... that will put us out there about dusk."

"Why wait so long?" Vince asked.

"I want to do this under cover of darkness... just in case somebody is watching."

"That makes sense," Clay said. He turned to Vince. "Y'all need to trust Carlos out in those mountains. Me 'n Roscoe know that from experience."

Carlos fetched a blanket from Lolita's cabin to wrap around the strongbox. When it was secured on the back of the pack mule, it looked merely like a prospector's bundle of supplies. He added a pick and shovel just to make it look more believable.

14

Vince Carter was a good companion on this trip into the mountains. He talked very little, and Carlos noticed that he kept watchful eyes in all directions. They had never been close friends; they had little knowledge of each other's personal lives. So when they stopped for water and nourishment mid-afternoon, Vince let his curiosity ooze out just a little. "I can see you're Mexican, but you speak like any white man, and you seem to have the savvy of an Indian."

Carlos was accustomed to strangers' confusion about his heritage. "I learned English from my white mother; Spanish from my Mexican father... but I was raised by Navajo..."

"Why were you raised by Navajo?"

"My real mother and father were killed... Apache raid... when I was nine years old. A Navajo family took me in, and I learned a lot from my Navajo grandfather."

"So... you've lived most of your life as a Navajo."

"Yeah, until Grandmother and Grandfather died a few years ago. But before that, they sent me to school in Yuma."

"So that's why you're so smart."

Carlos just smiled. "What about you, Vince?"

"Not much to tell, really," Vince replied. "I grew up in Dakota Territory... learned 'bout cattle ranchin' there. But I hated those cold winters. So 'bout five years ago I came here... to be someplace where the cows don't freeze to death in the winter. Nunes Ranch gave me a job... been here ever since."

Carlos and Vince had only been gone about an hour when Clay and Roscoe decided to walk around, maybe check on Buster at the livery stable. Fred was resting quietly.

It seemed highly unlikely that Belmont and his brother

would show up in town, but just knowing they weren't far away created an uneasy feeling. They would be harder to spot, now, as Fred had described their attire to be more like that of cowboys. They would blend in with the local populace, and at a distance, easily mistaken for ranch hands.

Buster brayed at Roscoe when he came near; it was, perhaps, his way of thanking Roscoe for bringing him to shelter, food, and water. Buster appeared to be healthy and satisfied, but not eager to pull a freight wagon just yet.

Just as Clay and Roscoe were leaving, Sheriff Gus Livingston and two deputies were dismounting their steeds outside the barn. "Clay and Roscoe," the sheriff greeted.

"Hello, Sheriff," Clay said. "Good to see y'all, and we're glad you're here."

"I didn't expect to see you boys here," Gus said.

"We came to help Carlos with the strongbox," Roscoe explained. "But things have changed."

"Where is Carlos?"

"He and Vince Carter are on the way out to the mountain now. They left a couple of hours ago."

The sheriff squinted, frowned, dumbfounded. "What... who..."

"We sure were surprised, too, Sheriff. Vince Carter is still alive. I thought y'all knew."

"But Belmont shot and killed him."

"Belmont shot and killed somebody else that *looked* like Carter," Clay said. "Believe me... Vince is alive and well."

"Then... who did Belmont kill?"

"Everybody thought it was Carter, but his face was tore up so bad... unrecognizable... they just assumed it was him."

"Well, that *is* a surprise," Gus said.

"But we've got some other big news," Roscoe said. "Thaddeus Belmont and his brother are somewhere close around here."

"How do ya know that?" Gus asked.

"Fred... the fellow who hauled the strongbox up here for y'all... got held up and robbed by two masked men yesterday... near Stone Cabin... he said it was Belmont and his brother."

"Fred told you that?"

"Yeah... he's here now... up in our hotel room sleeping. He rode one of his mules here to warn us."

"Is he okay? Is he hurt?"

Clay and Roscoe told all they knew about the hold-up; about Fred's bleeding wrist from being tied to the wagon; about Belmont stealing food from Fred's cargo; about Fred nearly collapsing from exhaustion.

"Then we all decided that Vince should go with Carlos out to the mountain, and me and Clay would stay here on the lookout for Belmont... and to keep an eye on Fred."

15

Just as Carlos had speculated, they approached the canyon where the strongbox was to be placed on the ledge a while after the sun had dipped below the mountain peaks to the west. In the deep valley between two mountains, the daylight faded quickly.

As they unloaded the blanketed strongbox from the pack mule, Carlos explained his strategy: "There's a ledge," he said as he pointed up the side of the cliff. "I'll take the rope up there and throw one end down. Tie the rope to the handle on the box, and I'll hoist it up."

Vince peered up the vertical rock wall. "How far up?"

"Maybe a hundred feet. The rope is a hundred and twenty feet long."

"I can't see anything up there," Vince said.

"That's the idea... nobody else can, either."

"How you getting up there?"

"There's a place where I can climb," Carlos said. "But it'll take me quite a while to get there... so just relax and guard the box 'til I throw the rope down."

Vince sat on the strongbox with the Winchester rested across his knees.

Carlos mounted his horse and rode toward the climbing steps. But he didn't stop there. He was headed around the mountain to the secret passage into the volcano basin. Deceiving Vince was necessary; Vince could not know that he had been to the secret hideaway, and it would be easy enough to explain the bow and quiver of arrows he was about to retrieve.

More than a half-hour had passed when Vince heard a voice calling to him. "I'm throwing the rope down now."

Vince jumped to his feet and looked up into the darkness. Carlos was just barely visible—merely a shadowy figure high above. Then the end of the rope appeared, descending toward him. When it was within reach, he grabbed it and tied it to the box. "All set," he called up to Carlos.

Within a few seconds, the box rattled against the rock wall and disappeared into the darkness overhead.

But before Carlos could bring the box all the way to the ledge, two gunshots rang out, echoing through the canyon, and both Carlos and Vince heard the slugs ricochet off the canyon wall, somewhere near, but impossible to discern in the darkness. With no warning, and at a time when Carlos was quite confident that he would safely complete the mission successfully, the sudden gunfire startled him and he lost his grip on the rope. The box fell, and he knew there was no stopping that much weight. He heard it slam to the ground below. The rope landed in a tangled heap next to Vince. Then he heard the sound of Vince levering a live round into the Winchester's chamber.

The box wasn't in place where they had intended, but now, that didn't seem important anymore. They had become targets, and Belmont—or his brother, Jules—had to be the shooters.

"You okay?" Carlos called out.

"Yeah," Vince replied. "Where did those shots come from?"

"Don't know... I'm coming down now." Carlos hesitated briefly, wondering if his movement could be seen by whoever was shooting at them. It was a chance he'd have to take. He cautiously inched his way along the ledge back to the rock climb; another shot echoed, but by the sound of the ricochet, the bullet had struck the wall somewhere in the vicinity where the box should have been placed. Apparently, the shooter couldn't see him. But he couldn't see where the shots were coming from, either. Carlos was quite certain, though, that it *had* to be Belmont. Who else would be shooting at them? He hustled down the rock climb, although, in the dark, it seemed a little more treacherous than it really was. Vince would be suspicious of the length of time he spent going up in comparison to coming down, but that, too, would have to be risked. Maybe he wouldn't even notice. Considering the present circumstances, getting on their horses and riding away was top priority.

Even in the dark, Carlos knew the way out. Vince didn't question the direction they headed; Clay had told him to trust Carlos, and he did. They weren't following the same way they came in, but Vince just kept an eye on the dark horse and rider leading the way. Carlos led him past the trail leading up to the key mountain; sure enough, just as he had suspected, two horses were tied at the mesquite trees there.

Away from the deep canyons where the moonlight started to give shapes to the surroundings, Vince noticed the arrows and a bow slung over Carlos's shoulders. "Where did that come from?" he asked.

"Oh... I forgot them up on the ledge last time we were here," Carlos lied. But he didn't mention the three gold nuggets in his pocket that he'd also retrieved from the basin.

"That had to be Belmont shootin' at us," Vince said after they were well away from the mountain.

"Yes, it was," Carlos replied. "Don't know how he could've gotten there that soon."

"Well," Vince said. "He had a good head-start."

16

Long after midnight, Vince and Carlos climbed the hotel stairs. Vince handed off the Winchester to Carlos and headed down the hall to his room.

Carlos, too, longed for his head to be on a pillow, but when he entered the room, lamps were lit and Clay, Roscoe, and Fred were playing Black Jack at the table. They all jumped up when they saw Carlos.

"How'd it go? Did y'all get the box on the ledge?"

"No... well... almost..."

"What happened?" Roscoe asked.

Carlos handed Fred his rifle. "We borrowed this for some extra protection in case we needed it."

Fred took the gun and cradled it in his arms.

"So, what happened?" Roscoe asked again.

"I almost had the box up to the ledge... then somebody started shooting at us in the dark."

"Who?"

"Couldn't see 'em... but my guess is Belmont."

"Rifles or pistols?" Clay asked.

"Sounded like forty-fives," Carlos replied.

"Where's Vince?"

"Went to his room."

"Did ya shoot back?" Fred asked.

"No... couldn't see where the shots came from."

Roscoe eyed the bow and arrows when Carlos tossed them in a corner. "You must've been to..." he stopped short and glanced at Fred, the one person in the room who probably didn't know about the secret hideout.

"Yeah," Carlos said, and winked at Roscoe. "I'm really tired. I want to go to bed. Can we talk about this in the morning?"

"But I hafta get back to my freight wagon," Fred said. "I'm leavin' tonight."

"No, you're not," Carlos snapped. "You'll leave in the morning... and I'm going with you."

"But... I'm already late... Bill 'n Angie will..."

"They know you're gonna be late. We sent word with the stage driver. With Belmont so close, you're not going alone. *I'm going with you.* Now go to bed so we can get up early."

Clay put a hand on Fred's shoulder. "Better do it, kid. I think he's right."

Fred grumbled a little, but then he took off his shirt and trousers and plopped into the bed.

Clay and Roscoe were the first to come down to the dining room for breakfast. Sheriff Livingston was already there. "G'mornin,'" he greeted them, and invited them to join him at his table.

"Mornin' Sheriff," they returned, and sat down.

"When do ya reckon Carlos will get back?" the sheriff asked.

"Oh... he and Vince got back late last night. He should be down any minute."

"So did he get the strongbox out there?"

"They ran into a little trouble..."

"What kinda trouble?"

Carlos and Fred appeared at the table. "We got shot at," Carlos said. "Okay if we sit with you?"

"Yes... by all means... sit down," Gus said as he gestured to three empty chairs. "You were shot at?"

"Yeah... I figure it was Belmont."

"Where did this happen?" Gus asked.

"At the ledge... when I was hoisting up the box."

"Either of you get hit?" Livingston asked. He was a bit shocked.

"No, Sheriff... we're both fine. They couldn't see what they were shooting at."

"So, where's the box now?"

"Not on the ledge," Carlos explained. "It fell back down. We didn't particularly want to stay there any longer, so we rode out of the canyon and headed back here."

"Did you have any guns with you?"

"Vince had his forty-five and Fred's Winchester."

"Did he return fire?"

"No... couldn't see where the shots came from... but there were two horses tied up by the trail to the peak where you arrested Belmont. They must've been up there."

Gus leaned back in his chair. "So... I reckon by now he's found out there's no gold in the box."

"That would be my guess," Carlos replied.

"Well then... not much point for my deputies to watch that place."

"They stole food out of my freight wagon," Fred added.

"Ah, yes," the sheriff said. "I meant to ask you about that.

Just exactly what happened? Clay told me they wore masks... how do you know it was the Belmont brothers?"

Fred explained the episode as it happened. And then he told about his previous experience of when Belmont failed to pay for his supplies at the mining camp. "That's how I know Belmont and his funny accent."

"And is your wagon and team still at Stone Cabin?"

"I sure hope so... Jonah was gonna look after it for me... I'm goin' back there now."

"And I'm going with him," said Carlos. "It'll be safer... hard telling where Belmont is by now."

"Good idea," Gus said. "I know it's Sunday, but outlaws don't take Sundays off. So I was hoping you could go with me and my deputies... show us the way to the mountain again... so we could pick up their trail. Couldn't Vince go with Fred?"

"I think Vince has to get back to his job at the ranch... he's got cattle to look after. Cows don't take Sundays off, either."

"I don't need *nobody* to go with me," Fred spoke up.

"Yes, you do," Carlos said firmly. "Belmont is dangerous... more dangerous now than you've ever seen him before. You know what happened a couple of days ago when you were alone."

"Yeah, but—"

"We could go with Fred," Roscoe said. "We've got guns—"

"Those derringer pea shooters might've gotten you outa one scrape with Belmont, but—"

Clay laid his .45 Smith & Wesson revolver on the table in front of him. "With all due respect, Sheriff... this ain't no pea shooter, and we'd have Fred's Winchester, too. Roscoe had one just like it back in Wisconsin. I think he knows how to use it."

Fred grinned. "My bedroll is in the wagon. You two need to bring yours. We'll be camping at least one night."

17

Fred kept a steady, rapid pace back to Stone Cabin.

"Better slow down some," Roscoe kept telling Fred. "Poor Buster will be too tired out again to pull the wagon."

Fred eased Buster into a slower walk, but gradually, they gained speed once more. "Can't help it," Fred told Roscoe. "I think Buster is anxious to get back to work... or maybe he misses Maggie."

Clay and Roscoe finally decided that the mule was in command; they just kept pace with Buster on their horses, ever watchful for other riders or anything else that seemed out of the ordinary.

"You know," Roscoe said to Clay. "Belmont is gonna think it was us who took the gold. *We're* the ones he'll come after."

"That thought occurred to me," Clay responded. "By now, he knows we're back. He's prob'ly got eyes and ears on the street, and he found out that the gold was still out there... just like the sheriff wanted."

"You're right," said Roscoe. "That's probably why he went back to the mountain so soon, thinking he'd get there before anybody else."

"Yeah... and now the sheriff's plan to catch him there red-handed kinda fell off a cliff."

"Maybe he'll just leave the territory... to avoid getting caught and going back to prison." Roscoe mumbled.

"Don't count on it," Clay replied. "He couldn't see it was Carlos and Vince last night in the dark. It's a good bet that he thinks it was us, 'cause we're the only ones who know where the gold is. If he thinks we've got the gold, which I think he does, he'll keep trying to get it."

"Maybe *we* should just leave the territory," Roscoe said.

"What? And miss out on all the fun of capturing Belmont... again?"

Roscoe starred at Clay. "Do you *really* think this is fun?"

"Well, y'all have to admit... it sure is exciting."

"Yeah, it's exciting, alright."

Clay seemed to thrive on this new-found adventure and the excitement it delivered. But even though Roscoe had faced off with Belmont and his gang once before—and defeated them —he still wasn't too certain of his desire for another encounter with a known killer. He and Clay and Carlos had taken risks, that their clever tricks would help them to overcome Belmont's brute force. And it had worked... that time. He had to admit to himself, though, that his and Clay's skill with their derringers, and the element of distraction that Carlos contributed, had made them the victors. Roscoe recalled how satisfying that had felt. Maybe Clay was right.

When they arrived at Stone Cabin General Store late that afternoon, Jonah was glad to see Fred again. "I was worried 'bout ya," he said.

"Awww... we made it just fine," Fred replied, as if it had been just a stroll among the cactus.

"How's the wrist?" the storekeeper asked.

Fred held out his left hand; he had removed the bandage that morning. "Still a little sore... but it's okay."

Jonah studied Clay and Roscoe a few moments. "Say... I remember you... you were on the stage a while back... stopped here for the night... on the way to Tyson Wells."

"That's right," Roscoe replied. "This time, we're escorting Fred... making sure he gets there safe and sound."

"Your wagon is out back, just like you left it," Jonah informed Fred. "I found an empty crate... put all those loose canned goods in... and the mules are in the corral... they ate up the last of your feed yesterday, so I gave 'em some hay this morning."

"Thanks, Jonah. I'll be out hitchin' 'em to the wagon so we can get on our way."

"Okay... but the Missus has a pot of beef stew cookin'... there's a stagecoach coming along soon." Jonah turned to Clay and Roscoe. "You two are welcome to have a bowl of stew, too."

18

"There's a lot of tracks here now," Carlos told the sheriff.

"Yep... goin' in all directions," Gus replied. He studied the empty strongbox, upright with the lid open, the rope still attached to one handle. "Is this how you left it last night?"

"No," Carlos said. "I think it was upside down... and the top was still closed."

"Well, then... we *know* that Belmont found an empty box."

Deputy Dan came back from investigating farther up the canyon. "Gus, there's tracks headed north out of the canyon," he said. "Looks like two horses."

Gus peered up and down the canyon. "There's only three ways out of here... south, north, and west." he said. "There's tracks to the south, but prob'ly all of those are ours from last week." Then he stared at the passage to the west. "Carlos and Vince came and left that way."

Carlos verified with a nod.

"I don't think they'd be heading south back toward Yuma," Gus said, staring in that direction. "So the tracks to the north are prob'ly the ones we should follow."

Deputy Albert returned from climbing up to the key peak.

"See anything up there?" Gus asked.

"Nope... nothin'."

Then the sheriff turned to Carlos. "Thanks for getting us out here," he said. "Now, it's your choice, son. You can ride with us... or you can ride alone back to Castle Dome."

Carlos didn't have to give it much thought. "I'll go back to Castle Dome."

"Okay... do you want a gun? I always carry an extra."

"No thanks," Carlos replied. "I'll be okay with my bow."

Gus just shook his head. *A Mexican with a bow and arrows*, he thought. He waved, and then he and his deputies rode off into the north canyon.

"Good luck," Carlos called to them. He waited until they were completely out of sight, long enough to be sure they didn't intend to return for any reason. Before he left, he wanted to be certain that Belmont had not accidentally stumbled onto the secret passage into the basin. He looked at the tangled rope heaped up beside the strongbox. It belonged to him; why not take it? It could be stashed at the hideout cave with his other belongings.

As he climbed toward the big boulders hiding the entrance to the basin, he realized that the sun was already getting low in the western sky. Perhaps it would be wise to just stay the night. Clay and Roscoe were escorting Fred on their way to Tyson Wells, and it would be at least another two days until they returned. *I'm on horseback now*, he thought. He could start out by noon tomorrow and easily make it back to Castle Dome before sunset. It seemed like a good opportunity to spend some quality time with Lolita.

No one had entered. Carlos was relieved that his secret was still safe, and confident that it would remain that way.

The early Monday morning air was crisp and cold; Carlos

was happy to just stay snuggled in his blankets, warm and safe in the little cave. He couldn't see the sky, but the dullness of everything he could see indicated that it could be a cloudy, dreary day ahead. It hadn't rained in a long time, and it was that time of year when rainy days weren't uncommon. Rain would be more than welcome.

He lay there thinking about Lolita Flores; *she would not be at the Flora Temple tonight, but at home in her cabin.* He hoped that he would be there with her. He could see her sparkling eyes smiling at him, and he could feel her soft, smooth skin and her long, silky black hair flowing over her shoulders. It seemed so real... then suddenly, another disturbing vision interrupted his thoughts—two masked bandits holding Fred at gunpoint. That image was quite real, too. He couldn't get it out of his mind.

He flipped the blankets off to his side and sat up, trying to focus more clearly. Clay and Roscoe were with Fred now; it was still early morning, and they would be getting close to Tyson Wells. He shouldn't have to worry.

19

The pace was slower now that Buster was regimented with the rest of the team again. The wagon wasn't quite so heavy since Jonah unloaded his lumber, so they were able to make good time.

Clay and Roscoe followed behind the wagon on the two spirited mares they had acquired at the Castle Dome livery stable. Roscoe still had Fred's rifle, and he knew that Fred seemed a little uneasy without it.

"How much money do we have with us?" Roscoe asked

Clay. They had left the bulk of their cash in the Vendome Hotel safe, as usual, retaining just enough for meals, lodging, and a little extra for unexpected expenses.

"Couple hundred," Clay replied. "Why do y'all ask?"

"I'm thinking that I should buy a revolver and a rifle... last time we were here, I saw Bill Scott has some in his store."

"Well, it's 'bout time y'all did that," Clay said.

Roscoe grinned. Since their discussion earlier that day about capturing Belmont, he had given serious thought to the many hazardous predicaments they had encountered, and he remembered telling Clay that *they are in a dangerous place.* Clay had always provided adequate protection. But now, considering the current circumstances, they may have suddenly become the targets of a greedy, heartless outlaw. For eighteen years, Belmont had continued his persistent search for the stolen gold; he knew he was close, and it didn't seem like he was about to give up anytime soon. He had murdered an innocent man in cold blood, and he would likely kill again. Roscoe and Clay could be sitting on a powder keg, and at any time they could be in the line of fire. The derringer had proven to be an impressive weapon, but it just wasn't enough now. *Yes*, Roscoe thought, he *should* have more effective firepower of his own to help even the odds.

Fred had run this route so many times, he knew all the good campsites. It was dark Sunday evening when he pulled the team into a thicket of trees. "We'll stay here," he told the others. "If we start out at dawn, we'll get to Tyson Wells before noon tomorrow."

They sat around a small campfire, enjoying the warmth it offered; the night air was chilly. Off in the distance, several spots of light— prospectors' campfires—dotted the mountain silhouettes. Coyotes yelped now and then. The sweet fragrance of creosote blossoms drifted through the night.

"Y'all lived here your whole life?" Clay asked Fred.

"As far back as I can remember," Fred replied. "But I wasn't born here. My father died from pneumonia when I was too young to remember... just after we came to America from Germany. Mom didn't have any kin in New York City, so she wrote a letter to Uncle Mike... he ran the store and stage stop here at Tyson Wells back then."

"The store that Bill Scott runs now?" Roscoe asked.

"Yeah... but it's moved since Uncle Mike owned it."

"So y'all came here when you were little," Clay said.

"Yeah... Uncle Mike picked us up at the Yuma train station and hauled us to Tyson Wells in his covered wagon... and he gave Mom a job takin' care of the boarding house."

"And you've been haulin' freight since..."

"Since before I was nine years old."

"How old are you now, Fred?"

"Fourteen."

Bill Scott couldn't have been any more relieved when he saw the mule team stop at the storefront at 11:00 o'clock on Monday morning, with Fred perched on the wagon seat. He didn't realize right away that the two riders were Fred's escorts, Roscoe and Clay, who had safe-guarded his arrival.

"The stage driver told me you'd be late," Bill said. "Did you have trouble?"

"You could call it that," Fred replied.

Clay and Roscoe dismounted, tied the horses to the hitching rail, and joined Bill and Fred on the board walkway. "Good to see y'all again, Bill," Clay said with a smile. "We came along to make sure he got here okay."

"Why? What happened?" Bill asked.

"I got held up day before yesterday... down by Stone Cabin."

166

"Held up? You mean... bandits?"

"Yeah."

"Who the devil would hold up a freight wagon?"

Clay stepped in. "Somebody who wanted food," he said. "We know who it was."

Bill stared at Clay questioningly.

"It was your old friend, Thaddeus Belmont."

"But... I heard he went to prison for murdering a cowboy over in Castle Dome." The *Wanted Dead or Alive* posters had not yet arrived, so Bill was unaware of the prison break.

"He did. But he escaped a few days ago, and now he's on the run with his brother."

Bill turned to Fred. "Are you okay? Did you get hurt?"

"Just a little rope burn," Fred replied. "I'm okay."

"Y'all should be proud of Fred," Clay continued. "He rode one of his mules all the way back to Castle Dome to warn us about Belmont."

"Why?"

"Well, we think he might be looking for me and Roscoe now."

"Why?"

"'Cause he thinks we're the only ones who know where the gold is that his gang robbed from a stagecoach... almost twenty years ago."

Bill was thoroughly confused. Clay and Roscoe explained while they helped unload Bill's merchandise from the wagon.

When he though he had a grasp on the story, Bill said, "So... the sheriff has the gold, but Belmont thinks *you* have it."

"That's about it. Except... there's ten bars still missing."

"I always thought Belmont was a little shady," Bill said. "But I never figured he was a murdering outlaw."

"Which is why I'd like to take a look at your gun selection," Roscoe said.

"Sure," Bill responded. "I have a few. What do you have in mind? Rifle? Shotgun? Revolver?" He walked them to a counter; behind the counter on the wall was a gun rack containing a variety of shotguns and rifles.

"I'd like a *good* revolver... forty-five caliber, and maybe a Winchester lever action."

Bill reached down and lifted a flat wooden box onto the counter top. "This is the best forty-five I have... the Colt Peace Maker." He flipped the hinged lid on the box. "Of course, I have cheaper pistols... like the prospectors buy... for snakes and coyotes and such... y' know."

"How about a Winchester carbine?" Roscoe asked. "You have one?"

Bill reached to the gun rack on the wall and pulled down the rifle. "Model ninety-four... best thirty-thirty there is... nickel-steel barrel." He laid it on the counter beside the Colt.

Roscoe picked it up. It looked good—a newer version of his old Model 73. It felt good in his hands. "How much for both?" he asked.

"Well, the Winchester is thirty dollars... and the Colt is twenty."

"How 'bout a holster for the Colt?"

Bill put a plain, brown leather holster on the counter. "This one is two dollars... the one that prospectors get... but I have a real nice one for five." He reached under the counter and produced an attractive polished ebony holster, hand-tooled with scrolls and roses, a genuine work of art.

Roscoe stared at it a moment, then picked up the Colt and slipped it into the stylish black holster. Perfect fit. His smile beamed emotional satisfaction. He looked at Clay; Clay nodded his approval. "We'll take all three... and a box of ammunition for both."

"Now Fred," Clay said as he and Roscoe were getting ready to travel. "Y'all be careful on your way back to Yuma."

"Sure, Clay," Fred replied. "Thanks for coming with me this time."

"If you want escorts again," Roscoe added, "we'll be happy to do it for you."

"Well, now that I have my rifle back, I'll be fine."

"Just in case, though, we'll either be at the Vendome in Yuma, or the Castle Dome Hotel."

"But you're goin' to Castle Dome now, right?"

"Yeah... we have to check on Carlos."

Roscoe felt a new sense of confidence and security with a revolver on his hip and a carbine in the saddle holster. Clay felt a little better about that, too; he hoped they didn't need the extra firepower, but it was good to have if they did.

About 1:00 o'clock, they started out. They'd had beefsteak and roasted potatoes at Scott's Stage Stop; canteens were filled with cool, fresh water. They had, at least, five or six hours of daylight, and with two good ponies under them, Castle Dome City was within reach.

20

Carlos didn't have a food supply with him now, so he speared a couple of trout from the creek, a tasty treat for his Monday morning breakfast.

Ominous storm clouds rolled across the sky and the smell of rain rode the wind gusts. His horse was tethered among trees where he would have some protection; it didn't seem to be a very pleasant time to start traveling just yet. Best to just wait it out. The storm would pass, and there would still be plenty of time to make the trip back to Castle Dome.

Within an hour, the tempest arrived in full force, and for two hours heavy rains continued to fall from the dark sky, driven by bursts of wind. Carlos was thankful that he had not ventured out, and grateful for the little cave that protected him from the torrents. He wondered about Clay and Roscoe and Fred; knowing Fred's routine, they probably camped somewhere between Stone Cabin and Tyson Wells, and Fred would insist on getting started again at first light. So that meant that they should be almost to Tyson Wells.

This storm seemed to be moving in that direction. Carlos hoped that Clay and Roscoe would take notice of the heavy approaching weather, and that they would not get in a hurry to start out for Castle Dome until it passed.

By noon, only sprinkles of rain continued on and off, and the wind had diminished to a steady breeze. Behind the storm, the sky was still cloudy, but brighter, and no longer showed any signs of more threatening conditions. Carlos had endured much worse; it appeared to be suitable for travel now.

He rolled up the saddle blanket, donned his poncho, arrows and bow, filled his canteen at the creek, gathered a big bunch of marsh grass, and headed down the mountain to his waiting horse. After a good rain, many of the arroyos would still have water flowing—rain water draining from the mountainsides —and ample water pools for the horse to drink.

From his own private stock, Sheriff Livingston had provided Carlos with a strong, healthy chestnut stallion— Caesar was his name—one that could easily go the distance, but he had been without feed—other than leaves and tufts of desert vegetation within his reach, and the grass Carlos gave him—so Carlos allowed him to plod along the rough terrain at his own pace, avoiding any undue stress to the animal.

After two hours, the horse didn't seem to be tiring at all, but Carlos dismounted and walked beside Caesar as they began an uphill climb where, at the top, they would pass by a low, jagged peak. After that, a long, gradual downhill slope would get them back on the low desert. From there, the trail crossed mostly flat land back to Castle Dome.

Halfway up the climb, Caesar whinnied and back-stepped as if he had been spooked by a rattlesnake. Carlos quickly scanned the immediate surroundings. *There were no snakes out in the open this time of year... it was too cold for them.*

"Easy boy... what's wrong, Caesar?" he said to the horse, as if he expected an answer.

Caesar whinnied again and nervously bobbed his head a few times.

It was then that Carlos saw the sinister-looking rider on a black stallion at the top of the hill. He froze for a moment, his stare focused. In an instant, he recognized the man—it was Thaddeus Belmont. Carlos felt his heart pounding and a breath caught in his throat. He thought, *how can this be?*

In the next instant, Belmont leveled his revolver toward Carlos and fired; the shot echoed in the mountain peaks. Carlos heard the bullet hit rocks behind him. There was nothing else to do now but get to cover. He grabbed Caesar's halter and together they sprinted to the nearest boulders off to his left, where he would be out of the gunman's line of sight.   Just before he was completely behind the rocks, he heard two more shots blast from Belmont's pistol, and then he felt the sharp sting at his side as one of the bullets grazed just below his ribs. He fell to his knees as Caesar trotted on farther. He knew he had been shot, but the wound felt more like the sting of a knife cut; he could see where the bullet had ripped through his poncho. But at that moment, there was no time to lift the poncho to examine the wound; he could hear the horse's hooves on the stones, coming closer.

Carlos stood, tried not to think about the pain, and readied his bow with an arrow, drew back the string, poised, his stiff left arm and arrow point aimed at the edge of boulders where he knew the rider would appear. He thought there was just one; he could hear no sounds of another.

"Where's my gold?" he heard the harsh Irish accent call out as the clicking of horseshoes on rocks came closer. He had nowhere to go. It was a matter of seconds until Belmont would be there, right in front of him.

Carlos remained silent.

"I know you have my gold," the angry voice said. "And I want it... now."

The black stallion's nose appeared first.

Carlos took a deep breath, held it, and hoped it wasn't his last. He prepared himself for the worst.

As the stallion and its rider came into full view, Carlos heard one more blast from the .45; he saw those menacing eyes and the twisted snarl, but by then it was too late. In that split second, the arrow pierced the breast of Belmont's coat. Belmont flinched, froze like a bronze statue for a moment, then fell limp from the saddle to the ground.

"Don't shoot the piano player," Carlos said softly as he stared at Belmont. Instinctive reactions had already brought another arrow to the bowstring, but Thaddeus Belmont was not moving. Thaddeus Belmont was not breathing. Thaddeus Belmont was dead.

The black horse sidestepped only a few feet away and stopped. Carlos listened for another horse, or perhaps, someone on foot, but there still wasn't any sound of other hooves or boots on the stones. It seemed unusual that Belmont was alone.

For a moment, Carlos thought it was a little odd that he felt no remorse, but then the burning sensation at his side reminded him that he had acted in self-defense. He recalled that day on the mountaintop, when Belmont had every intention of killing him, Clay and Roscoe, and he would have, had they not outsmarted him before he made his move.

Carlos thought he might be facing more trouble now, but at least he was still alive.

21

Clay and Roscoe had been riding about two hours; they weren't far from Stone Cabin. To the south, where they were headed, they could see dark thunderheads forming, and the prevailing winds seemed to be pushing the clouds their way. With a little luck and sure-footed mounts, they hoped to reach the Stone Cabin General Store ahead of the storm. They also hoped that Jonah Yarber sold rain ponchos at his store, as they weren't exactly prepared for such weather.

Without any warning, from behind some mesquite trees ahead on their right bolted two riders, bandannas covering their faces, pistols drawn. They stopped, facing Clay and Roscoe, blocking the trail.

Roscoe instinctively pulled the Winchester from the saddle holster and Clay drew his revolver; they came to a halt only fifty feet from the other riders. There was no doubt in their minds who these men were. "What do y'all want?" Clay called out to them.

"Where is the gold?" the Irish accent said.

Because their mouths were covered, Clay wasn't sure which one was talking, and the voice didn't sound exactly like Belmont's, but maybe it was the mask that made it sound differently now. "We don't have the gold," he replied.

"But I think you know where it is."

"Actually, we don't," Roscoe said.

Then the other masked man spoke: "I will kill your Injun friend if you don't bring us the gold... and then I will kill you."

A sudden thunder clap and lightning flash startled the horses; they began turning, jumping nervously, swinging and bobbing their heads in a chaotic manner.

"Bring us the gold," one of the men shouted, "Or your friend will die."

Then a huge, dusty whirlwind nearly obliterated Clay's and Roscoe's vision; sand and grit stung their faces and they couldn't breathe. Both their hats were whisked from their heads and sailed into oblivion. For a few seconds, it seemed that the world would end. The two mares instinctively trotted out of the twister, away from the swirling dust and sand, where it was possible to breathe again.

When they were able to clear the grit from their eyes and regain some sense of orientation, the two mysterious riders were gone; they, too, had dashed away from the whirlwind... and to parts unknown.

They holstered their firearms; the impending threat had left with the wind. It wasn't far away, but Clay and Roscoe both thought they were out of immediate danger... for the time being. However, the thunderstorm was still approaching rapidly; for the moment, getting to Stone Cabin was top priority. They kicked their heels into the mares' flanks, urging them into a full gallop. The general store wasn't far.

Rain had started falling when Jonah Yarber welcomed them into his establishment. "You boys made it just in time," he said. "There's a dandy storm comin' this way."

"Yeah, we know," Roscoe responded. "We've been watching it for the last couple of miles."

"And we got caught in a dust eddy that claimed our hats," Clay explained. "Hope y'all have some hats in your store."

"And some rain ponchos," Roscoe added.

"Well," the storekeeper replied. "I've got some hats... not the style you wore, as I remember... and I've got some oilcloth dusters... but I don't think you fellas should be thinkin' 'bout goin' back out in that storm just yet."

"No, we'll prob'ly wait it out for a while," Roscoe said. "But we hafta get back to Castle Dome City as soon as possible."

"What's yer hurry? Ain't no more stages due 'til tomorrow mornin' so I got plenty o' room... you fellas should think 'bout stayin' the night... we'll get your horses in the barn... let this storm pass."

"But, you see, Jonah..." Roscoe said. "We just got ambushed by the same two varmints that robbed Freddy last week."

Jonah's eyes widened. "Did they rob ya?"

"No... that twister saved us... but they threatened to kill our friend, Carlos... so we hafta get back there right away."

"Carlos? The fella that rides with Fred sometimes?"

"Yeah... that's him."

"How do you know it was the same men? And why would they want to kill Carlos?"

"We've had dealings with that bunch before. They think we have the gold they robbed from a stagecoach twenty years ago."

Jonah seemed a little overwhelmed; Clay explained what had happened on the mountaintop when Sheriff Livingston arrested Thaddeus Belmont.

The storekeeper stepped behind his counter to retrieve a sheet of paper, then held it up for Clay and Roscoe to see. "This arrived on the mornin' stage," Jonah said. "I just ain't got around to puttin' it up yet."

"Wanted dead or alive," Clay read aloud the bold print.

"One thousand dollars reward for the capture of Thaddeus Belmont... escaped from the Yuma Territorial Prison." Belmont's picture was at the center of the page.

"Well, how 'bout that?" Roscoe said. "Now we won't get in trouble if we shoot the bastard."

"Yeah," Clay replied. "Now, let's get the horses in the barn before the storm gets worse." He glanced at Jonah. "Then we'll take a look at those hats."

22

Sheriff Livingston was already back in Castle Dome City when Carlos arrived late Monday afternoon, still riding Caesar, and a black stallion in tow. Slung across the saddle on the black stallion was Thaddeus Belmont's body. Carlos noticed familiar horses tied in front of the sheriff's little office not far from Castle Dome Hotel; he headed right to it.

Livingston saw Carlos through the front window, rose from his desk chair and went to the door.

"Buenos Dias, Sheriff Gus," Carlos said.

"Buenos Dias, Carlos," the sheriff returned.

"I didn't expect to see you back here so soon," Carlos said.

"We lost the trail up around King mine... too many tracks goin' every which way up there." Caesar was partially blocking Gus's view of the black stallion; he didn't notice the body right away. "What ya got there? You pick up a stray?"

"No, Sheriff." Carlos handed the black stallion's reins to Gus. "He's yours now. And if you want to lock me up..."

"Now, why on earth would I want to lock you up, Carlos?"

Carlos turned his head and stared back at the body on the stallion, and then pointed. "That's why."

Livingston stepped around to where he could see the body slung over the stallion. "What the..." He stepped closer. "What happened, Carlos? Who is this?" He was staring at the backside of the body.

"That's Thaddeus Belmont," Carlos replied. "I'm sorry... I had no choice... he shot me once, and he was going to kill me."

"You didn't have a gun... you told me."

"No... but I had this," Carlos said. He took the bow from his shoulder and handed it to the sheriff. "I put his gun back in his holster. He shot at me four times... I shot one arrow."

Livingston stared at the bow in his hands, unbelieving.

By then, Deputy Dan had come out see what was going on; he walked around to the other side of the stallion where he could get a good look at Belmont's face. "Yep... it's Belmont, alright," he said to the sheriff.

"So... am I in trouble?" Carlos asked. "Are you gonna lock me up?"

Gus stepped to the other side next to Dan and saw that the body was, in fact, Thaddeus Belmont. He reached up and pulled Belmont's .45 from the holster, flipped open the loading gate and slowly spun the cylinder, dumping the cartridges into his left hand. "Four empty shells, two live," he said to Dan.

"I had to pull the arrow out of his chest," Carlos said. "To get him over the saddle."

"You said he shot you," Gus said, looking Carlos in the eyes.

Carlos lifted his shirt, exposing the wound.

"We'd better have Doc Hull take a look at that," Gus said. "Dan, go tell Albert to fetch the Doc."

"It's just a flesh wound," Carlos said.

"Well, we'll have the Doc look at it anyhow."

"Should I take Caesar back to the livery stable?" Carlos asked.

"We'll take care of Caesar," Gus replied. "You just go inside and have a seat... wait for Doc Hull."

Carlos dismounted from Caesar and walked into the Sheriff's Office. Deputy Dan guided him to a chair. He sat there waiting, watching through the front window as Gus and Dan untied the rope and pulled Belmont's body off the stallion's back. It seemed odd that they had left him unguarded, as he was sure that his next move would be into the jail cell beside him.

Doc Hull arrived a few minutes later; he always kept his horse and buggy hitched and handy in case of emergencies, and in a mining camp, there were frequent emergencies. The aging doctor had provided medical services in Castle Dome for a long time; he had treated every kind of injury from broken bones and smashed fingers and toes to powder burns and snakebite. When he heard *gunshot wound,* he wasted no time to get there.

He rushed into the Sheriff's Office and looked around the small room and in the jail cell. Then he turned to Carlos. "Where's the fella with a gunshot wound?"

"That would be me," Carlos replied. He lifted his shirt. "It's just a graze... but Gus insisted that you come."

The doctor knelt on the floor beside Carlos to get a better view of the injury. "Well, that don't look too bad," he said. "But we don't want it to get infected." He opened his black case, got out a bottle of clear liquid and a cloth, and began swabbing the wound. When he was almost finished applying ointment and a bandage, Sheriff Livingston walked in and sat in his desk chair.

"Keep that bandage on for three or four days," the Doc instructed Carlos. "You'll probably have a scar, but I think it will heal up real nice."

"Thanks, Doc," Carlos said.

Doc Hull smiled warmly. "You come see me if it starts causing you any pain." He closed his case and left.

Carlos sat quietly watching the sheriff writing something in a journal at his desk. "So... should I go in the jail cell now?" he asked impatiently.

"No," Gus replied. He scribbled a few last words, and then turned to Carlos. "That was a pretty good shot... with the arrow, I mean."

"I didn't mean to kill him..."

"But you did."

Carlos frowned, tilted his head down and stared at the floor. "So... am I going to prison?"

Gus picked up a sheet of paper from his desk. "These were apparently sent on the stage from Yuma yesterday. This one was slid under my door." He stood, stepped across the room to where Carlos sat, handed him the paper.

Carlos stared silently at the *Wanted* poster a few moments. Then he looked up at Gus. "Dead or alive?"

"That's what it says," Livingston replied. "And that poster is official... from the Yuma Territorial Prison."

"So... what happens now?" Carlos asked.

"Well, for starters, I'm sending Dan and Albert back to Yuma with the body and my report that identifies you as the captor... and then, in a few days, I'll take you to the Yuma courthouse and we collect your reward."

23

The Monday storm had lasted too long for Clay and Roscoe to start out for Castle Dome City, so they stayed the night at Stone Cabin. When they left Tuesday morning, they had hats —not their usual style—and because the sky was still quite overcast with suspicious, dark clouds, they bought the dusters, just as a precaution.

With the thought of being watched, and the ever present possibility of another ambush, the ride back to Castle Dome seemed to take longer than it actually did.

"D'ya think they know where we're going?" Roscoe asked.

"Yeah, I'm almost sure they do," Clay said. "And it's a good bet they know exactly where Carlos is, too."

"But Carlos could still be with the sheriff..."

"I doubt it," Clay said. "He doesn't want any part of being a lawman... he said so himself. He led them out to the mountain, but no... he didn't go with them after that."

"You're prob'ly right," Roscoe admitted. "He's prob'ly at Lolita's cabin right now."

"It wouldn't surprise me."

Roscoe glanced at Clay. "You look funny in that hat."

"So do y'all," Clay replied with a grin.

Vince Carter saw the two riders coming on the northwest trail, but he didn't recognize Clay and Roscoe with their new wide-brimmed western style hats until they were within shouting distance. He was on his way into Castle Dome, too, herding four steers to the butcher shop. He waved.

Clay and Roscoe caught up with him and slowed their pace to his. "Y'all bringin' the miners some beef?"

"Yep," Vince said. "New hats, huh? They look good."

"Yeah, the wind blew ours away in that storm yesterday."

"Did ya' get Fred to Tyson Wells okay?"

"Sure did... and then *we* got ambushed by those scoundrels on the way back. The storm drove 'em away, though, and we stayed at Stone Cabin overnight."

"I thought Sheriff Livingston was gonna be hot on their trail..."

"I'm afraid the sheriff is a long way behind the Belmont brothers," Clay replied. "Y'all gonna be in town for a while?"

"By the time I get these critters in the corral it'll be close to suppertime," Vince said. "Yeah, I'll stay tonight."

"Okay... we're gonna go find Carlos now. See y'all later at the hotel saloon... I'll buy y'all a beer."

Castle Dome Rock, high on the mountain watching over the town below like a sentry, had been visible for many miles, but with dark, gloomy clouds stretching from one horizon to the other, the well-known landmark's reddish luster was absent. When the Castle Dome Hotel came into their view, Clay and Roscoe felt relief from the menacing thought that the Belmont brothers could be watching their every move. But here, the escaped convict wouldn't dare be seen. By now, there would be more of the Wanted posters circulated, and the entire population of Castle Dome, perhaps, would be aware of the killer at large.

Just as they expected, one of the Wanted posters displaying Thaddeus Belmont's face had been tacked to the wall beside the Hotel entrance. Clay stopped to briefly look at it once more. "Y'all go in and get our room," he said to Roscoe. He glanced at the sheriff's little office building. "Looks like the sheriff might be back... I'll go tell him about Belmont up at Stone Cabin."

"Howdy, Sheriff," Clay said as he entered the office.

"Well, hello Clay," Gus returned. "I like your new hat. Good to see you again... did you get Fred back to Tyson Wells?"

"Yes we did," Clay replied. "But y'all might want to know that we saw Belmont up near Stone Cabin on the way back here yesterday. They tried to ambush us, but the windstorm got the better of them."

"No, Clay... you didn't see Belmont yesterday."

"But I'm sure it was him... he had a mask on, but the Irish accent and..."

"Belmont is dead," Gus interrupted. "My deputies are on the way back to Yuma with the body right now."

Clay's eyes widened and his jaw dropped.

"Your buddy, Carlos brought him in yesterday afternoon slung over the back of a horse... dead as a barn pole. He'd shot him with an arrow. But it was in self-defense... Belmont shot him first."

"Carlos got shot?"

"Just a graze... Doc Hull fixed him up... he'll be okay."

"Where is he?" Clay asked.

"Don't know for sure... maybe in a room at the hotel... poor fellow thought he was going to prison... he didn't know about the reward."

"So... who were those two men at Stone Cabin?" Clay asked.

"Belmont was alone, according to Carlos," the sheriff replied. "If one of them had an Irish accent, then I s'pose it could've been his brother, Jules. But I don't know who the other one might be."

"One of the gang we wounded up on the mountain?"

"Not likely," Gus said. "They're all still in the Yuma jail."

"Well, those two... whoever they are... are still lookin' for the gold. They threatened to kill us if we didn't give it to them."

"Trouble is," the sheriff said. "Jules ain't wanted, so I don't have any justifiable cause to arrest him."

"So, what are we gonna do?" Clay said, discouraged.

"Well, I'm gonna take Carlos to Yuma to collect his reward. I think when Jules finds out Thaddeus is dead, this might all be over. Oh, and by the way, we found out the identity of the cowboy Belmont killed... his name was Luke Prescott... family owns a ranch over by the river... his father put up the reward money."

Clay returned to the hotel; Roscoe was waiting for him in the lounging area. "Someone just checked out," Roscoe said. "The maid is getting the room ready for us... and Carlos ain't here."

Clay sat down on the sofa next to Roscoe; his solemn expression was difficult for Roscoe to interpret, but something was definitely troubling him.

"Why the long face?" Roscoe asked.

"Carlos shot Belmont with an arrow yesterday... on the way back from the mountain."

"What?" The statement didn't register completely.

"Apparently..." Clay began. "Belmont ambushed Carlos... shot him... and Carlos killed him with an arrow."

Roscoe just stared a few moments, trying to translate the words into an image. "But we saw Belmont at Stone Cabin yesterday."

"Must've been his brother, Jules... and some other hombre... the sheriff didn't know who it might be."

"Where's Carlos? Is he hurt bad?"

"No... guess it's just a graze... not bad... don't know where he is... I thought he might be here."

Roscoe seemed stunned. "Belmont is really dead?"

"Yeah... Sheriff's deputies are on the way to Yuma with the body."

"S'pose we should look for Carlos?"

Clay thought a moment. "No," he replied. "He'll find us."

24

At the supper table that evening in the hotel saloon, Vince asked, "Did you find Carlos?"

"No," Clay replied. "We decided not to look after we found out about his encounter with Belmont."

"He must be pretty good with that bow," Vince commented.

"Yeah, he is," Clay said. "I've seen him pick off a rabbit at thirty yards."

"Will you two be leaving the Territory now?"

"This ain't over yet," Clay said. "Those two hombres who ambushed us over at Stone Cabin sounded too serious."

"But the gold is gone... the sheriff has it, right?"

"They don't know that," Roscoe said.

"I hope y'all can understand this, Vince," Clay said. "Carlos is a good friend, and we can't just leave knowing he could still be in danger. Jules Belmont still holds a grudge against him... even if he doesn't get the gold, and when he finds out that Carlos has killed his brother, he'll have even more reason to do him harm."

"Maybe Carlos should just stay away from here," Vince suggested.

"Not likely," Roscoe replied. "He has a sweetheart here... remember?"

"The sheriff is still after Jules, ain't he?" Vince said.

Clay shook his head. "Jules isn't wanted for anything. Gus told me he doesn't have any *justifiable cause* to arrest him."

"Seems to me," Vince said after some serious thought. "We need to find Carlos and warn him about all this."

They finished their supper and determined the most likely place to to begin the search for Carlos—the Flora Temple Bar. Chances were good that he would seek Lolita's company at a time like this, and if she was working, Carlos might be there, too.

As usual, a crowd of miners occupied the Flora Temple, among them, many Mexicans. But there was only one Carlos; his colorful serape and well-groomed onyx black head of hair stood out, even with his back to them. Clay, Roscoe and Vince zigzagged through the gathering to where Carlos sat on a stool at the end of the bar, his fingers wrapped around the handle of a half full beer mug. Clay and Roscoe sidled up to the bar on either side of him.

Carlos glanced to one, then the other; a hint of a smile formed on his lips. "I'm glad you're here," he said. "Wasn't sure when you'd get back."

"We just got here this afternoon," Clay said. "Got caught in a storm at Stone Cabin... stayed there last night... rode here today."

Carlos stared briefly at the new hats.

Roscoe explained. "Ours got blown away in the storm, and these were the only ones that Jonah had that fit proper."

Carlos nodded his approval with a friendly grin.

"We know what happened," Clay said. "Sheriff Livingston told me all about it."

Carlos took a sip of his beer, then stared at the mug on the bar. "I never killed a man before."

"I understand how y'all feel," said Clay, his hand on Carlos's shoulder. "But it was self-defense..."

"And Belmont got what he deserved," Roscoe added.

"I know," Carlos said; he looked Roscoe in the eyes. "I have never been afraid to die... my Navajo Grandfather taught me that long ago."

"And what did your Grandfather Spirit tell you now?"

Carlos smiled, perhaps because Roscoe and Clay sincerely respected his feelings and his beliefs. "That I have so many reasons to stay alive, that my life has a purpose, and that Belmont didn't have the right to end it." He turned to Clay. "I feel no remorse for what I did."

Lolita appeared behind the bar. "Welcome back," she said to Clay and Roscoe. "I like your new hats... very becoming of you." And then she acknowledged Vince, as well. Her radiant beauty and warm smile were stunning. "There's an empty table over there." She pointed. "Go sit down... I'll bring you some beers."

When they were settled around the table, Lolita brought the mugs of beer. She brushed her hand across the back of Carlos's neck in a caressing manner as she left, not difficult for the others to notice.

"Carlos," Clay said. "I know y'all have a lot on your mind right now, but there's something important we have to talk about."

Carlos recognized the urgency in Clay's voice and directed his attention to him.

"Yesterday," Clay began, "we were ambushed, too, near Stone Cabin. We thought it was Belmont... the Irish accent and all. But it must've been his brother, Jules... and some other fellow... we don't know who."

"They still think we have the gold," Roscoe cut in.

"Did they shoot at you, too?" Carlos asked.

"No," Clay replied. "A big whirlwind kicked up, and all we heard was that they would kill our *Injun friend* if we didn't bring them the gold."

"Next thing we knew," Roscoe continued, "when we got out of the whirlwind, they were gone."

"The thunderstorm was just about on us," Clay went on. "So we rode on to Jonah's place fast as we could."

"Did ya know about the reward on Belmont's head?" Carlos asked.

"Not until Jonah showed us the poster... that's the first we knew of it."

"By *Injun friend*, we figured he must mean *you*, Carlos."

"They called me Injun the night I spied on their camp, the night I shot Jules in the leg."

"Livingston seems to think that this is all over now," Clay said. "But that little run-in we had at Stone Cabin makes me think that it's not."

25

Tyson Wells was growing. More prospectors pouring into the region from other parts of the country meant the need for more supplies, more stores, hotels, boarding houses, and more saloons. It was about to get a new name, too. Years before, its post office had been closed and moved to Ehrenberg, twenty miles distant at the river, where the steamboats delivered the mail. But now that the town had become more established, with more people who didn't fancy the idea of hiking twenty more miles to receive their mail from loved ones and friends back home, a new post office had been approved, but the old name could not be applied; it had to be changed. Angela Scott suggested the name "Quartz Site." Another rule stated that a village name could only be one word, so Quartzsite became the new name for the post office.

Fred Keuhn's freight business was expanding, too. He couldn't always wait for the weather to clear; Fred and his mules were toughened to inclement conditions. He was halfway to Yuma to pick up another large load of goods when Carlos and Sheriff Livingston left Castle Dome, headed for Yuma, as well.

Carlos had already indicated that he intended to return to Castle Dome City soon after he had collected the reward and deposited it in the bank. Clay and Roscoe decided to ride to Yuma, too, so that Carlos would not be traveling alone on the return trip. They would stay at the Vendome until Carlos had completed his business and was ready to travel.

Not far from Yuma, they came upon Fred Keuhn and his four mules plodding along the trail, his wagon loaded with empty nail kegs and barrels with various stenciled labels—Beer, Flour, Whiskey, Crackers—all to be refilled for a future journey into the mining districts.

Clay noticed right away that Fred's Winchester wasn't wrapped in a blanket, hidden away, but perched on the seat beside Fred. He nodded his approval.

"Nice hats," Fred commented.

Carlos trotted Caesar up alongside the wagon. "When will you be headed back?" he asked Fred.

"In a day or two," Fred replied. "Got a lot of orders to fill... lot of merchandise to pick up."

"Anything goin' to Castle Dome?"

"Prob'ly will be."

"I have business to attend to, but I'll find you and help you get loaded as soon as I can," Carlos said. "We'll ride with you back to Castle Dome."

"You goin' to collect your reward?" Fred asked.

"How'd you know 'bout that?"

"Heard it from a stage driver yesterday."

Carlos didn't like leaving Fred behind, so he kept pace with the slower mules. But the sheriff didn't want to slow his pace to that of the freight wagon all the way back to Yuma. Livingston was confident that Fred was in safe territory, and he was certain there would be other important matters waiting for his attention at his office.

"We'll stay with Carlos and Fred, too," Clay told the sheriff. "We have no reason to be in a hurry."

"Suit yourselves," Gus replied. He waved and rode on.

Although he was accustomed to traveling alone, Fred was delighted to have the company on this trip. Carlos jumped into the wagon, tied Caesar to the back, and took a seat beside Fred. Riding close beside the wagon, Roscoe noticed Carlos holding the Winchester. "You should have one of those," he said.

"Never really thought I needed one," Carlos replied.

26

After two days in Yuma, Fred's wagon was loaded with larger than usual quantities of various store goods and saloon beverages. Sheriff Livingston had accompanied Carlos to the Court House to collect the reward money, which Carlos quickly deposited in his bank account. Clay and Roscoe were well-rested, with their usual bowler hats that they found at the local Haberdashery.

Before they started the journey back to Castle Dome, Carlos had one more item of business to conduct. "I'm quite fond of Caesar," he told the sheriff. "I'd like to buy him from you."

Gus Livingston had always liked the Mexican boy who had been raised by a Navajo family; he had watched him grow, and he admired Carlos for the respectable young man he had become, despite his star-crossed past. "I've seen how that horse has taken a likin' to ya," Gus said. "He was a mustang from New Mexico... broke and trained by the best. You look quite cavalier on his back. I think you should have him."

Carlos beamed a broad smile. "How much?" he asked.

Gus rubbed his chin, thinking. He looked at Carlos and saw the joy in his eyes. He gazed at Caesar in the stable stall. Knowing that the animal would be well-cared for, he said, "I won't sell him to you. Let's just call it a gift... from me to you, Carlos... for all the help you've been to me... but you'll have to get your own saddle."

Carlos was overwhelmed. "Thank you, Sheriff Gus."

"Shall I go with you to the tack shop for a saddle?"

"Just a halter and a blanket will do," Carlos replied. "Bareback is how I learned to ride."

Early the next morning, Fred's mules were harnessed and hitched when Clay and Roscoe came to the livery stable. Carlos brushed Caesar as if he were preparing him for a circus performance. "He's mine now," he told them proudly. Caesar whinnied and bobbed his head.

"Congratulations, but where's your saddle?" Roscoe asked.

"Don't have one... don't want one," Carlos replied. "I'll be riding bareback now, the way I learned."

What seemed to be a slow and tedious pace to Clay and Roscoe, was normal to Fred, and Carlos had become atoned to the lack of speed by virtue of the several trips he had made with the young freighter in the recent past. The journey to Castle Dome would take all day—two more to Tyson Wells. To Fred, that was just the natural course of things.

The first half of the distance to Castle Dome twisted through sand dunes and hills, so many places for road agents to launch a surprise ambush on unsuspecting travelers. During the time on that part of the trail, three stagecoaches—two northbound and one southbound—passed by, among other wagons and buggies and one of the huge ore wagons drawn by forty mules. Occasionally, men on horseback and prospectors leading a burro or two and numerous people on foot came along. Clay and Roscoe kept vigilant watch on and off the road for anything suspicious, in particular, the two riders they had recently encountered. But they saw nothing that posed any danger.

The dunes and hills gave way to a broad plain, the Castle Dome Mountains to the east, and the Trigo Mountains to the northwest, less chance for bandits to be hiding. On the fourth stop to afford the mules some rest time, Fred suggested that they should eat: "I have plenty for us all," he said as he dug out the provisions. He'd picked up some extra dried beef, biscuits, and beans when he found out the other three would be joining him for the trip.

Carlos tethered Caesar to the back of the wagon and rode beside Fred the rest of the way to Castle Dome. It was too late to deliver the crates of goods to the Mercantile, but not too late for the barrel of Kentucky Whiskey to be taken to the back door of the Flora Temple Bar.

The usual nighttime crowd had gathered at the popular watering hole, drinking to relieve the stress from a long day in the mines. Clay, Roscoe, Carlos, and Fred had spent a long day on the trail, so when the whiskey barrel was unloaded and rolled into the Flora Temple back room, Clay suggested they partake of some cool refreshments in the front room before retiring to the hotel. The idea was well-received.

Rather than sitting down at a table right away with the others, Carlos perused the barroom in search of Lolita. It was a Saturday night... she should be there.

Another barmaid brought drinks to the table. Fred felt like a king sipping his beer among friends. Clay and Roscoe were grateful to wash down the day's dust.

Clay noticed a man sitting at a table across the room; he thought the man looked vaguely familiar, but he couldn't connect the face with a name. He pointed out the man to Roscoe. Roscoe didn't recognize him.

"That kinda looks like Mr. Sanderson," Fred offered, "Yuma Hardware." He had picked up freight from there several times.

"What's he doing here?" Roscoe asked.

"Prob'ly selling nails to the Mercantile and horseshoes to the blacksmith... that I'll prob'ly haul next trip."

Carlos came back to the table. He seemed distraught.

"Didn't y'all find Lolita?" Clay asked.

Carlos shook his head. "No." He sipped his beer. "She hasn't been here for two nights."

"Maybe she took ill," Fred said.

Carlos gulped down his beer. "I'm gonna check her cabin."

"Should we go with y'all?"

"No... take care of your horses and mules," Carlos said. "I'll meet you at the livery later."

27

Carlos was already at the livery barn taking care of Caesar when Clay, Roscoe and Fred arrived. His disposition had not improved.

"Was Lolita at her cabin?" Roscoe asked. In the dim kerosene lamp light, he saw Carlos shake his head.

"Where could she have gone?"

"I don't know," Carlos replied. By the sound of his voice, the others knew he was worried. "She would have left word if she was going away... I'm sure of it."

When the two mares were in the stall, and the four mules were turned out into the corral, Clay, Roscoe and Fred joined

Carlos in the ring of light cast by the lantern hanging from a post near the center of the barn.

"Could she be with friends... or relatives?" Clay asked.

"Lolita has no family here," Carlos said. "And she doesn't ever speak of any close friends."

Then, from a dark corner of the barn came a startling voice that sent chills racing down their spines. "Your lady friend is not far away." The very distinct click of a pistol hammer being cocked immediately followed.

Clay was the only one at a vantage point to see the dark, shadowy figure near the rear door of the barn. But it was only a vague silhouette. The circle of light given off by the lantern where they all stood didn't quite reach the corner and the mysterious shape of a man. He knew it wasn't Jules Belmont... no Irish accent, but he thought it could be Belmont's companion from that day at Stone Cabin.

"Any one of you so much as move a hand toward a gun... I'll drop you where you stand," the voice said calmly, but in a commanding tone.

Fred tried to swallow the lump in his throat.

"What do y'all want from us?" Clay said.

"I want the gold you took from that strongbox on the ledge." There was certain anger in the voice.

"We don't have it," Clay said.

"I don't believe you."

"That's the truth," Roscoe blurted out. "We don't have it."

"If you don't get that gold to me..." the man said with even more anger, "I will bury your Mexican sweetheart's bones behind the barn... right next to that stage driver I put there eighteen years ago... where the horses will trample down any sign of a grave, and no one will find her... ever."

"Where's Lolita now?" Clay demanded.

"That's not for you to know... but she's safe... Jules is

guarding her."

Carlos could no longer remain silent. The thought of Lolita with that hateful, disgusting man made him cringe. "I'll bring you the gold... if you let Lolita go unharmed."

All heads turned to Carlos.

"Now we're getting somewhere," the gunman said. "But you have it kinda backwards... I'll let Lolita go when you bring me the gold."

"How can I trust you?" Carlos growled.

"Well, now," the man replied. "That's a chance you'll have to take."

Clay or Roscoe didn't know what Carlos was scheming. Perhaps it was just a means of buying some time. They both knew that Lolita meant more to Carlos than anything else in the world. But whatever his plan involved—*if there was a plan*—they would back him to the end.

"It'll take me a day to get it," Carlos said. "I can have it here by tomorrow night."

There was a brief moment of silence. "You have twenty-four hours," the man said. "Be here at ten o'clock tomorrow night... with the gold. We'll be here with your lady friend. And no funny business, or Lolita will never serve another drink at the Flora Temple."

There was no more discussion. They heard the door hinges squeal, and then the door gently bumped against the frame.

Clay drew his revolver and took a step toward the darkness, but Carlos grabbed his arm and held him back. He knew the necessity of avoiding any actions that might jeopardize Lolita's safety. Clay wrestled himself free and went to the door, cautiously, slowly pushed it open. There was nothing to see but Fred's loaded freight wagon and the mules in the corral. Everything else was just motionless shadows in the moonlight.

"What are you thinking?" Roscoe asked Carlos. "That you're gonna give him a gunny bag full of rocks?"

"No," Carlos said. "I'm gonna give him the gold."

Clay returned from the doorway. "And just how are y'all gonna convince the sheriff to turn it over to y'all?"

"Don't have to," Carlos replied.

Even in the dimness, Clay and Roscoe could see a calculating mind at work. They allowed him a few moments to think.

"Do y'all have any ideas about where they might be holding Lolita?" Clay asked. "We could go looking for—"

"There's some abandoned prospectors shacks around," Fred interrupted excitedly, trying to be helpful.

"Clay... Roscoe..." they heard a whispering voice call to them. "It's me... Vince Carter... up in the loft."

They looked up, only to see a pair of boots starting down the ladder.

"What are y'all doing up there?" Clay asked.

"When the hotel is full, Johnny let's me sleep up here." He continued down the ladder to the barn floor. "I heard everything... I'll do anything I can to help."

"Carlos has a plan... I think..." Roscoe said.

"What are ya gonna do?" Fred asked, frightened excitement in his voice.

"Fred," Carlos said. "Will you be here 'til tomorrow night?"

"Well... sure... I guess so... tomorrow is Sunday... I can't deliver my freight here tomorrow. It'll hafta wait 'til Monday."

"Good," Carlos said.

Roscoe's curiosity couldn't wait. "Is this another one of your *don't-shoot-the-piano-player tricks?*" he asked.

"No," Carlos said. "Better than that. Will you and Clay ride with me tomorrow?"

"Of course," Clay said. "Y'all can count on us. Where are we going?"

Carlos didn't want to answer that question right then. "I'm gonna stay at Lolita's cabin tonight. Meet me in the morning at the hotel for breakfast."

"But you and Fred should stay with us at the hotel tonight," Roscoe said. "It would be safer for you."

"No," Carlos replied. "I need some time alone... to talk with the Spirits."

28

"Ya know," Fred said when he, Clay and Roscoe were back in the hotel room, "that sounded kinda like Mr. Sanderson... the Yuma hardware man."

Clay had been thinking the voice was the same as the masked man with Jules Belmont at Stone Cabin. He looked squarely at Fred. "Are y'all sure about that?"

"Well, I can't be absolutely sure... but it did sound like him."

Clay thought a while. Sanderson was in town... Fred had identified him at the Flora Temple, so it *was* possible. Then, like fireworks streaking across an ink-black sky, the vision exploded in Clay's head. He turned to Roscoe. "Do y'all remember? The hardware fellow in Yuma... when we first came here. Sanderson... Jim Sanderson... he acted a little strange when he got a good look at the map... remember?"

The memory of the storekeeper gradually came into focus for Roscoe. "Yeah, I kinda remember..."

"He told us he was a Wells Fargo agent at the time of the robbery."

"Yeah, now I remember," Roscoe replied. "He asked if we found anything else besides the map."

"And didn't Thaddeus Belmont admit... up on the mountain, just before the sheriff got there... that he had an agent friend who told him when and where the gold shipments were going?"

"Yeah, you're right," Roscoe said.

"Now that Thaddeus is dead," Clay went on, "he's trying to capitalize on what Belmont failed to do. Sanderson is the only other person who knew the particulars about the hold-up... 'cause *he's* the one who destroyed the Wells Fargo records."

"D'ya think he really killed that stagecoach driver... like he said?" Fred asked.

"Maybe," Clay replied.

"The stage driver was the only one who could've identified the hold-up gang," Roscoe added.

"I wonder what Carlos has up his sleeve," Clay said.

"I don't know," Roscoe responded. "But I'm sure we'll find out in the morning."

Early Sunday morning, there were fewer patrons in the hotel dining room; most of the miners were still sleeping off Saturday night's indulgence. Those who maintained better judgment were congregating at the church. Carlos joined Clay, Roscoe and Fred at their table about 8:00 o'clock. He seemed rested and calm, but it was certain that he harbored a magnitude of concern. The only words he spoke were to the barmaid to order his breakfast.

Clay finally broke the silence. "We figured out who that man is... Jim Sanderson... Yuma Hardware."

Carlos made eye contact with Clay. "It's possible."

"Well," Clay said. "Did y'all know he was the Wells Fargo agent back in eight-five?"

Carlos just shook his head.

"Me 'n Roscoe talked to him the day after we first met y'all.

Jack Dunne at the Ruby Saloon suggested that he might be able to help us with the map."

Carlos stared at Clay, waiting for him to continue. Clay went on to explain that first meeting with Sanderson in his store and their summation as to the role he now played in the current situation. "My guess," Clay went on, "is that Thaddeus Belmont *wasn't* the mastermind behind the robbery... like everybody thought. It was Sanderson."

Carlos took it all in, gave it thought. "But that doesn't change what we have to do now," he finally said.

"What *is* your plan?" Roscoe asked.

Carlos looked at Roscoe, then Clay, and then he turned to Fred, who was just taking the last bite of his breakfast. "Will you go to the stable and see what Vince and the stableman are doing? I saw them out by your wagon."

Fred swiped the cuff of his shirt sleeve across his lips. "Sure," he said. "Should I tell him—"

"Just go," Carlos interrupted.

Fred arose from his chair and headed to the door.

"I didn't want to tell you this in front of Fred."

Clay and Roscoe gave their full attention.

Carlos lowered his voice. "We'll ride out to the mountain this afternoon to get the gold bars," he explained.

"What gold bars?" Clay asked. "The gold bars are in a bank in Yuma."

"Not all of 'em," Carlos said.

Clay's jaw dropped. Roscoe's eyes widened.

"When you left on the train... headed for Texas... I took the next stage to Castle Dome City to see Lolita. But before I spent time with her, I went out to the mountain."

A curious little grin appeared on Roscoe's face.

"I found the trail leading up to the ledge, and I removed ten bars of gold from the strongbox."

"What did y'all do with 'em?"

"They're hidden at the basin... with Grandfather's gold... where no one will ever find them."

"But... why—"

"I did that for you." His eyes danced from Clay to Roscoe several times. "You had risked your lives to keep it from falling into the wrong hands... and you would've gotten nothing of the treasure you worked so hard to find."

"So, y'all had the missing ten bars all along."

Carlos nodded. "I would've gotten it all for you and left the empty box on the ledge, but I never got another chance to go back again before Sheriff Gus asked me to help *him* find it."

Roscoe reached across the table and put his hand on Carlos's forearm. "Carlos... I am deeply touched by your kindness towards us... you are a good person at heart," he said. "Why didn't you tell Livingston... when he discovered part of the gold was missing?"

Carlos looked Roscoe in the eyes. "He never asked me."

29

"You ain't gonna believe this!" Vince exclaimed when he and Fred walked briskly to the table. He was covered with dust and dirt from his shoulders to his boots.

Fred sat down in the chair he had vacated earlier. Vince sat down next to him.

"What?" Clay asked, urging Vince to lower his voice.

"When Johnny got to the stable this morning... 'bout sun up... I told him 'bout that fella tellin' you 'bout burying that stage driver out back."

All eyes from around the table were focused on Vince.

"Well, Johnny knew right where to look. He'd noticed a soft spot in the ground... 'n he'd filled it in a couple of times... long time ago. So, we got shovels and started digging." He opened his right fist to reveal a badly tarnished gold pocket watch. "We found this among what appears to be part of a leather coat... most of it is rotted away." He pried open the the watch cover. There, engraved on the inside of the cover was the name *J. H. Dawson.*

"All you found was a leather coat?" Roscoe asked.

"Oh... no... there's bones, too... a whole skeleton."

All faces turned solemn. Apparently, Sanderson wasn't bluffing—unless he was claiming for himself the outrageous acts of others, and that didn't seem likely. Lolita Flores had been kidnapped. Now that it was known who was partnered with Jules Belmont, perhaps the plan that Carlos had conceived would change. Obviously, the plan would almost certainly include some violence, to a degree; maybe Carlos would think differently, now that it involved a well-known and respected Yuma merchant.

"Does this change your plans at all?" Roscoe asked.

"No," Carlos replied. "I don't care who it involves. It just adds a couple of things to the list."

It was agreed that Vince and Johnny would continue to retrieve the remains of Mr. Dawson from the shallow grave, wrap it in a canvas, and hide the canvas in some obscure corner of the livery until the sheriff arrived. The grave would be filled in, and Fred's wagon parked over it.

"While Roscoe and Clay ride with me to get the gold," Carlos explained, "Vince and Fred will take a message to the telegraph office to be sent to Sheriff Livingston in Yuma. It will say that we have discovered the bones of J. H. Dawson, possibly the stage driver of the 1885 hold-up, possibly murdered by Wells Fargo Agent Jim Sanderson, and that he should check the Wells Fargo records for those names. It will also say that Sanderson is here now, and that he and Jules Belmont have kidnapped Lolita Flores." He glanced at Vince and Fred. "We'll have it all written out for you."

"That means the sheriff won't get here until tomorrow," Clay said.

"That's right... so we can't depend on his help tonight," Carlos replied. "*We* have to do this."

Everyone at the table listened carefully to Carlos as he laid out the rest of the strategy. "Me and Clay and Roscoe will come back at ten o'clock. We will go directly to Fred's freight wagon behind the livery. That's where we will negotiate the exchange—the gold for Lolita's release. Fred and Vince should already be hiding in the loft, quiet and out of sight, in case something goes wrong."

Fred and Vince nodded their acknowledgment. Everything was in place. Everyone knew what they were to do, where they should be, and when to be there.

As they were leaving the dining room to make all the necessary preparations, Carlos discreetly grabbed Fred's arm and whispered in his ear, "Make sure, without fail, that your Winchester is loaded and in easy reach under the wagon seat."

"Okay... will do," Fred agreed.

30

Sheriff Livingston was at his office catching up on some paperwork when the messenger delivered the telegram. He read it... then he read it again. He took a couple of minutes to put everything in perspective. Carlos had authored the message; Gus trusted him. Apparently, the matter of the 1885 stagecoach robbery wasn't completely resolved. The Dawson name didn't come to mind; as he thought about it, no stage driver had ever come forward, to Gus's knowledge. The driver's disappearance would account for one more measure of hiding any identity of the bandits.

But part of the information in the telegram didn't make sense; he had just seen Jim Sanderson at his store yesterday afternoon. It didn't seem possible that he could be at Castle Dome City and have orchestrated a kidnapping since then. Yes, Sanderson had once been a Wells Fargo agent, but in Livingston's opinion, he was not a murderer or kidnapper.

"Dan," Gus called to the deputy who was in charge of the jail for the day. "I want you to check Jim Sanderson's house... see if he's there. Then, see if Abe Sims is at the Wells Fargo office. If he's not, find him and tell him I need to see him there as soon as possible."

"Do you need to talk to Sanderson as well?" Dan asked.

"Not right now," Gus said. "Just see if he's home."

More pieces of the puzzle had surfaced, like a forgotten pair of old boots falling from a dusty closet full of cobwebs. It could be quite certain that gun-slinging gambler, Clay Edwards, and his partner, Roscoe Connor were part of the scenario; they had encountered Jules Belmont and another man—they now presumed to be Jim Sanderson—who had threatened Carlos. If Carlos was in company with Clay and Roscoe now, he had plenty of competent protection. As for the kidnapping of Lolita Flores, Gus could only assume that it must be Belmont's way for getting to Carlos. But why? The gold was no longer within his reach.

A half-hour had passed when Deputy Dan returned. "Jim Sanderson is sitting in the porch swing with his wife," he reported. "Abe Sims will be at the office within the hour."

"There aren't any coaches arriving this afternoon," Abe Sims explained. "That's why there's no one here in the office today." He unlocked the door and accompanied the sheriff into the back where the archived record books were stored.

"We need to look for this name," Gus said. "J. H. Dawson... he was possibly the driver of the stage held up in eighteen eighty-five."

"But... Sheriff... we didn't find any record of that," Sims said.

"Look at earlier records... to see if his name appears on other trips."

Sims pulled down two volumes from the shelf and began paging through the trip records. During the month prior to the January hold-up, he found several entries that he pointed out to Gus. "Driver," the sheriff read aloud. "John Henry Dawson. That must be him."

"Is that what you needed to know?" Sims asked.

"Let's look to see if he ever worked after the hold-up."

Sims paged through two months of trip records, but Dawson's name did not appear.

Livingston had been just a young deputy at the time of the robbery. He remembered riding with the posse, and the shoot-out in the Chocolate Mountains, and capturing Victor Flores the next day. But he couldn't recall any concern shown at the time for the coach driver's whereabouts. Most of the drivers were single men, with no families, so if he had disappeared, no family would be looking for him. All of the gang members had been killed or jailed, so the lawmen weren't looking for the driver for the purpose of seeking identity information. Dawson simply vanished, and no one really cared.

31

The reply telegram sent to Carlos from the sheriff only found its way to a pigeon hole mail slot at the Castle Dome Hotel. When it arrived, Carlos, Clay, and Roscoe were many miles away collecting the gold bars from a low cavern at the basin. They would not see the message that informed them that the sheriff and his deputies would be on their way to Castle Dome at first light the next morning.

When the gold was packed into the saddle bags, Carlos looked at his pocket watch. "We have time," he told Clay and Roscoe. "I'll get some fish from the creek... while you make a fire at the cave."

While they waited for the fish to roast over the fire, Roscoe asked Carlos, "Do you think just ten gold bars will satisfy Belmont and Sanderson?"

"I'll have to convince them the sheriff has the rest."

"What if they don't accept that?"

Carlos didn't have an immediate answer, but by the look in his eyes, Roscoe and Clay both knew they should be prepared for a fight.

"Do you consider me a thief?" Carlos said. "Now that you know why ten bars of gold were missing from the strongbox?"

"No," Clay replied. "I believe y'all had good and honest intentions. If what y'all told us was true, then it wasn't for selfish reasons."

"I would not lie to you," Carlos said solemnly. He peered at each of his companions with absolute sincerity. "I am grateful that you are the best friends I have known since Grandfather died. One of the most important things he taught me was to be loyal and honorable to my true friends; they are more valuable than any other worldly possession."

"We feel the same about you," Roscoe said. "That's why we will do all we can... take risks if we need to... whatever it takes to help you get Lolita back safely. After all, we're prob'ly the reason she got mixed up in this trouble. We owe you this."

Clay nodded his full agreement.

Darkness had swallowed up the landscape by the time they rode into Castle Dome; a bright, full moon was rising over the mountaintops, and soon everything would be bathed in the silvery light. Carlos had been mindful of the time during the entire journey; with fifteen minutes to spare, he hoped that Vince and Fred had secreted themselves in the livery barn loft. And he sincerely hoped that Lolita was still alive and unharmed.

Most of the town was asleep, but yellow streaks of light spilled from the Flora Temple Bar windows and the tinkling melody from the piano cut through the stillness. The smell of smoke drifted from a few chimney pipes on a gentle breeze. It was not unlike any other late night at Castle Dome, yet, to Carlos, Clay, and Roscoe, there seemed to be an eerie anxiety in the air as they rode slowly past the closed and dark business places.

As they rounded the corner past the hotel and rode to the rear of the livery stable, they knew they had arrived at the point of no return, face to face in a confrontation that bore no rules. Carlos dismounted from Caesar and stood beside Fred's wagon. He quickly surveyed the area; beyond the livery stable was nothing but open plain from there to the mountain, where, in the moonlight, he could see the road leading to McPherson Pass.

As Clay and Roscoe dismounted from the mares, two men emerged from the shadows without warning, taking Clay and

Roscoe and Carlos completely by surprise. One of them was holding Lolita in front of him; her hands appeared to be bound behind her back. And there was no mistaking their two revolvers aimed at Clay and Roscoe.

"Well, now," the Irish accent spoke. "You fellows are right on time."

With their hands held out to the side, to clearly show they weren't holding any weapons, they faced the kidnappers. "We like to be punctual," Clay said with sarcasm.

"Where's the gold?" Belmont demanded.

Clay pointed with his left hand. "It's in our saddlebags."

"Okay," Belmont said. "But first... you're gonna throw down them shootin' irons," he ordered. "And the rifle in your saddle holster, too," he said to Roscoe.

Clay and Roscoe laid their revolvers on the ground, and Roscoe reached for the Winchester. He laid it on the ground beside his pistol.

"Now those derringers you got hid up your sleeves," Belmont said. His brother had warned him.

Clay and Roscoe shook loose the derringers and laid them next to the revolvers.

"Now... step back away from the guns," Jules barked.

They complied and glanced at each other; they were unarmed... defenseless... helpless.

Carlos painfully watched Sanderson force Lolita to take a few steps forward, his gun still trained on Clay, as Jules carefully advanced to the array of weapons on the ground.

Belmont took a long, scrutinizing look at the three standing before him to make sure they had no other weapons. "Now, get those saddlebags down here so we can take a look at that gold," he snarled.

Clay and Roscoe cautiously stepped back to their horses, slipped the saddlebags off, carried them to where Belmont stood, dropped them to the ground.

Belmont knelt, his eyes and his revolver still on Clay. He waved the gun, signaling them to move away. When Clay and Roscoe took a couple of steps back, Jules unbuckled the four flaps one by one and flipped them open. From his shirt pocket he withdrew a match and struck it on one of the buckles. It flared brightly for a few seconds, and then diminished to a normal burn. Jules moved the match from one compartment to another until he had seen the contents of all. "There's only ten bars here," he growled. "Where's the rest of it?"

"That's all there is," Carlos said. "Sheriff Livingston has the rest."

"How do I know you ain't tellin' a lie?"

"It's the truth," Clay said. "I saw it at his office in Yuma."

"I oughta shoot the bunch of ya," Belmont snarled.

"And bury us beside J. H. Dawson?" Clay responded. He dangled the tarnished gold watch he had taken from his coat pocket.

His response caught Belmont off-guard. He turned to look at his partner.

"I was wondering how long it would be 'til someone found that," the man holding Lolita said. "That ain't Henry Dawson that you obviously must've dug up."

"Then... who is it?" Roscoe demanded.

"Don't know," the man said. "But that's my watch. I put it in his pocket hopin' that someone would find it... but about eighteen years sooner."

"You're J. H. Dawson?" Roscoe asked.

"That's me... John Henry Dawson."

Carlos studied the man holding Lolita. Same height, same build as Jim Sanderson, and in just the moonlight, his facial features even resembled Sanderson. But he *wasn't that man.*

"You see," Dawson said. "I wanted the lawmen to stop looking for me. I planned the hold-up and arranged for the bars to have no identification. After the robbery, I brought the coach back here... killed that drunken cowboy and buried him with my watch."

"And what about Thaddeus Belmont?"

"He was my front man..." Dawson said, "so I didn't have to be seen in public. But Thaddeus was an idiot, and he made a few mistakes, didn't he?"

Jules scooped up all the pistols, put them in the saddlebags, then picked up Roscoe's Winchester. "Turn the lady loose, Henry," he said. "Let's get outa here while we can."

Jules lugged the saddlebags to two horses waiting in the shadows, and then walked them to where Dawson and Lolita stood. Dawson watched him until his horse's reins were within grasping range. He pushed Lolita forward and swiftly mounted the steed. Lolita stumbled and fell, unable to maintain her balance with tied hands.

Carlos ran to Lolita, helped her to stand, and nearly carried her to the side of the wagon. "Are you hurt?" he asked her quietly.

She only sobbed, and couldn't speak.

Carlos knew what that meant. Without any hesitation, he reached over the side of the wagon to beneath the driver's seat. The feel of cold steel was reassuring. In one smooth but rapid action, the Winchester rifle was at his shoulder, leveled and aimed toward the McPherson Pass road where the two riders loped their horses across the desert. "You should've picked a darker night," he said, and pumped the lever action, fired. Pumped again, fired again.

Roscoe and Clay watched in awe as the two riderless horses continued to trot toward the road.

Carlos put the rifle down and immediately untied the

restraints holding Lolita's hands. He hugged her tightly a few moments, then turned to Clay and Roscoe. "Round up those horses and get your saddlebags back," he said, and to Lolita, "Don't cry... you're safe now."

Fred and Vince scurried out the livery back door, their mouths gaping, speechless. They had watched the entire event through cracks between the barn boards.

Clay and Roscoe were still in a state of confused awe. Clay listlessly pointed toward the open desert, and then toward the Winchester leaning against the wagon wheel. "But... y'all said..."

"I said," Carlos replied, "that I didn't feel the need for one. I never said I didn't know how to use it."

32

Two weeks had passed since Clay, Roscoe, and Carlos had finally brought an end to the Belmont gang. Although there had been bloodshed, there seemed to be a comforting relief, knowing that the scoundrels responsible for so much unrest had been delivered to their just rewards.

Fred had resumed his usual freight schedule without the worry of road agents making his travel hazardous. But his exposure to the criminal realm and the encounters with Clay, Roscoe, and Carlos had inspired him; he dreamt of the day when he would be old enough to take a position as a lawman... perhaps Constable at Tyson Wells... or, Quartzsite, as the town was now to be called.

Sheriff Gus Livingston had requested that Clay and Roscoe remain in Yuma while he waited for the Territorial Circuit Judge to make an appearance. There was still the matter of the gold and its theft that had been on the books for nearly two decades. No one had come forth to make any claim as to its ownership, and because so many mines and smelters had closed since the robbery, it was impossible to determine its origin. In all fairness, indisputable decisions should be made by the court.

There were no lawyers present in the courtroom the morning the judge had scheduled a meeting to review the facts. There were no defendants, no plaintiffs, no jury. Only the sheriff, his deputies, Abe Sims representing Wells Fargo, the bank president, Clay Edwards, Roscoe Connor, and Carlos Volero were there.

"As I understand it," the judge began, "this stagecoach robbery was all faked, that the driver—John Henry Dawson—was the lead conspirator."

"It is my belief," Sheriff Livingston said, "that is correct."

"Is it also correct that all persons involved in the alleged hold-up are now deceased?"

"Yes, Your Honor," Livingston replied.

"And do I understand correctly that you have been unsuccessful in determining the origin of the gold?"

"Yes, Your Honor... all the records had been expunged. The only identification we discovered was the Wells Fargo name engraved on the strongbox when the gold was recovered."

"Well," the judge said. "That doesn't prove anything. If the box had been engraved with *George Washington*, that wouldn't prove that it belonged to him. Wells Fargo never *owned* that gold, but was merely charged with its transport."

Everyone in the room was silent. It had been assumed that the gold would be turned over to Wells Fargo, without any doubt.

"Now," the judge went on. "*Who* actually found the missing gold?"

Sheriff Livingston stood up to speak. "Your Honor, the gold

was actually located by these three young men." He pointed to Clay, Roscoe, and Carlos, and voiced their full names.

The judge stared at the three a few moments. "You all appear to be too young to have been involved with the original event. How did it happen that you discovered this gold?"

Clay stood. "We... Roscoe and me... found a map, hidden in an old book, sir, and we decided to come here to look for the lost treasure."

"And where were you when you found the map?"

"In South America. But the book came from a shop at a mining camp in Montana."

"Where are you from?" the judge asked Clay. "You sound as though you come from Rebel country."

"Woodville, Mississippi, sir. Hometown of Jefferson Davis."

"And you?" The judge pointed to Roscoe.

"My father runs a mercantile in Wisconsin."

"And did you bring Carlos with you from South America?"

"No, sir," Roscoe replied.

Carlos arose from his chair. "I have lived in Arizona Territory all my life. My parents were killed by Apache. I was raised by a Navajo family here in Yuma."

The judge was astonished by the perfect English that Carlos spoke, but he didn't ask the reason for it. "What is your connection with Mr. Edwards and Mr. Connor?"

"I helped them find a hotel... and we just became good friends. They needed a guide out in the desert."

"According to Sheriff Livingston's report," the judge continued, "it was you who fired the shots that brought down Jules Belmont and John Henry Dawson. Is that correct?"

"Yes, sir."

"Why did you do that?"

"They were running away after they stole Clay's and

Roscoe's guns..." Carlos paused a moment to clear the lump in his throat. The rest was painfully difficult for him to say. "And after they kidnapped and raped Lolita Flores."

The judge turned to Sheriff Livingston. "Has Lolita Flores been properly cared for?"

"Yes, she has, Your Honor," Gus replied. "Doc Hull examined her and treated the minor injuries she sustained."

The judge had heard enough. He leaned back in his chair, reviewed the notes he had scribbled during the discussions, and then descended into deep thought.

Everyone sat quietly.

After a few minutes, the judge sat up straight and said, "Earlier, Sheriff Livingston imposed upon me to rule on the disposition of the gold, and to determine how much of its worth—if any—should be distributed as reward for its recovery. I find it quite difficult to arrive at such a figure. However, considering all the facts and circumstances, I *have* reached a decision. Because there is no proof of legal ownership, I do declare, in my official capacity as Territorial Circuit Judge, that the entire amount of gold is now the property of those who found it, just as the gold a prospector finds is legally his." He looked directly at Carlos, Roscoe, and Clay. "Gentlemen... you will distribute the proceeds of your find among yourselves in denominations as you see fit. The banker will see to the transaction."

The missing ten bars of gold would remain a mystery to the sheriff to his dying day. Carlos naturally refused a share of the $64,000 that Clay and Roscoe tried to give him. "I already have my share," he told them, as the ten missing bars were safely tucked away. But he would be forever grateful for their generosity.

It was a day reminiscent of when Clay and Roscoe boarded

the eastbound Southern Pacific back in January. They were, once again, saying farewell—but not goodbye—to a friend they knew could never be equaled.

"Where will you go this time?" Carlos asked while they waited for the train to arrive.

"We've talked it over," Roscoe said. "Clay and I agree that we should spend some time with our families again. They've only seen our letters for a long time."

"So I'm going to Natchez, Mississippi for a while... have a mansion built for my folks... maybe even try my hand at some poker on a river boat," Clay said.

"And I'll be back at Baraboo, Wisconsin... having a mansion built for my folks... and fishin' at Devil's Lake," Roscoe added.

"And when we get tired of poker and fishin,' we'll meet in St. Louis," Clay continued. "We'll figure out what part of the world we want to see next."

"And we both expect wedding invitations."

Carlos grinned. "Count on it."

ABOUT THE AUTHOR

J.L. Fredrick has called Wisconsin home for most of his life. But retirement in 2012 changed all that. Now, living full-time in a motor home, he travels the US, and home is wherever the motor home is parked.

He grew up on a Wisconsin farm and attended a one-room country elementary school, and then rode a bus to High School in town. After college in La Crosse, Wisconsin, he spent some time with Uncle Sam during the Viet Nam era.

He entered the transportation industry in 1974 as an over-the-road truck driver. In later years, he served as Safety and Personnel Management for several trucking firms in Minnesota and Florida. Eventually, he moved back to Wisconsin.

His writing career overlapped other employment. By the time he retired in 2012, he had 15 novels and two non-fiction history volumes published. Now there are 22 titles.

He presently continues to tour the country, writing still an important part of his life. This novel is the result of spending many winters in Arizona.

Made in the USA
Monee, IL
19 March 2023

29769933R00125